His eyes were very kind, his expression sympathetic.

Then he reached out and tucked Kaycee's hands into his strong ones. This time she didn't move. Suddenly it didn't seem at all strange to let him touch her. It was there again. That warm feeling of being cared for. Being looked after.

If his long arms closed about her she would be able to lean on him and he would never let her down.

Ridiculous. She'd only met Rowan this morning. She didn't even know the man!

Mary Hawkins lives with her minister husband and two of their three grown children in the Hunter Valley north of Sydney, but still thinks of herself as a Queenslander! She is a registered nurse who returned to her profession several years ago after a long break and found tremendous changes in the medical world. Now her love of nursing has been surpassed by her love of writing, but close contacts in the medical profession help keep her stories current and real to life.

TRUSTING DR SCOTT

BY

MARY HAWKINS

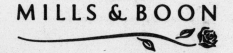

MILLS & BOON

*All the characters in this book have no existence outside the imagination
of the author, and have no relation whatsoever to anyone bearing the
same name or names. They are not even distantly inspired by any
individual known or unknown to the author, and all the incidents are
pure invention.*

*MILLS & BOON, the Rose Device and
LOVE ON CALL are trademarks of the publisher.
Harlequin Mills & Boon Limited,
Eton House, 18-24 Paradise Road, Richmond, Surrey TW9 1SR*

© Mary Hawkins 1996

ISBN 0 263 79802 X

*Set in Times 10 on 11¹/₂ pt. by
Rowland Phototypesetting Limited
Bury St Edmunds, Suffolk*

03-9609-47621

Made and printed in Great Britain

CHAPTER ONE

KAYCEE slammed her car door and winced. That had not been a good idea. For a moment she leaned against the little car and closed her eyes, which hurt in the early morning spring sun.

'Why can't it be a dull, grey morning? Even a fog would do instead of this sun,' she mumbled out loud. She rubbed the back of her neck and then glanced at her watch. Ten minutes late already. Hurriedly she straightened and her stomach lurched again.

She moaned softly, wishing fervently that she had rung in sick after all. 'Oh, no, I thought that last bout *was* the last!' she muttered, leaning against the car again.

Usually Kaycee enjoyed the first couple of hours of the early morning shift, especially on a Sunday. Unless there had been emergency admissions in the last twenty-four hours the atmosphere in the wards would be relaxed, with more quality time to spend with the patients.

But this morning was very different.

After a sleepless night she had managed to fall into a deep sleep at dawn. When she woke she found that she had forgotten to set her alarm. Then she had discovered that in all the turmoil of the last twenty-four hours she had forgotten to iron her only clean uniform. So now, as well as still feeling nauseous, her head was throbbing and her heart felt like lead.

As she took a deep breath and started across the car

park a red sports car swept into a space closer to the casualty entrance. She glanced back as she reached the main door and noted with a flash of interest that a tall man had alighted and stood looking about him. He saw her and started forward but she hastily shoved open the door and slipped inside.

'Sorry, man,' she muttered. 'I'm too late already; you'll have to read the signs to Cas.'

When Kaycee at last strode into the ward office she was officially fifteen minutes late—more than half an hour later than her usual arrival. The other nurses stared at 'always-early-Kaycee' with surprise. The night sister, Jill Lawe, was an old friend from school-days. She grinned sympathetically.

As she murmured a quiet apology Kaycee avoided their eyes, knowing how different she must appear from her usual neat-as-a-pin, cheerful, professional self.

The morning shift sister in charge of the medical and surgical patients looked up at her, her mouth open to deliver a reprimand to Kaycee for being so late. She stared and then her mouth closed with a snap and settled into a grim line. Kaycee groaned inwardly. Surely her appearance wasn't so bad that it made even young Sister Brooks speechless!

Kaycee had hoped that some miracle had taken place on the drive to the hospital and her eyes wouldn't be as bloodshot and her face as pathetic as it had been staring back at her from her bathroom mirror.

The RN scowled ferociously. 'Nurse Wiseman, how dare you—?'

'I *must* finish this report, Bronwyn,' the night sister snapped. 'I need my bed. Now, about Mr Rodgers. . .' Jill Lawe continued firmly to finish her report.

Kaycee threw her old school friend a grateful glance

but she knew that she was going to cop crisp words of disapproval, if not worse, some time during the shift.

As Jill closed the last file she added abruptly, 'Sally rang last night to say that John Swain has raced off, leaving Doctor Gordon's new locum to take any calls. She was worried because Ian Taylor had already gone and the new bloke was later than expected. He had not turned up before John took off.'

At the general murmur of disapproval she added drily, 'Yeah, officially it's Doctor Swain's mother this time. Oh, and that IVAC is playing up again.' Jill stretched wearily. 'Had to take it off and do regular checks on Mr Sanders's drip flow rate the last couple of hours.' She sighed and rose to her feet. 'Well, I suppose it made me realise how much time these IV automatic control machines save us.'

Kaycee frowned. Mr Sanders's name was on her list of allocated patients. So now her time would be taken up checking the drip rate every half-hour. 'No spares around?' she asked hopefully.

'Only one in Cas and they wouldn't lend it in case of an emergency,' Jill said with a scowl.

As the other nurses began to disperse Kaycee grabbed the files on her patients whose reports she had missed and began to scan quickly through them.

'Nothing new for you, Kaycee,' murmured Jill softly in her ear as she picked up her belongings next to her. 'Mr Sanders's diarrhoea and vomiting stopped late yesterday and he's responding well to the antibiotics. Just keep an eye on that drip, though. And how about you? You look—' She broke off as Bronwyn Brooks bustled over.

'There's no time for socialising, Nurse. Get started on your showers and beds.' Sister Brooks paused as

Kaycee closed the file and rose to her feet. 'I want to speak to you later,' she snapped. 'And do something about that hair!'

Kaycee murmured her 'Yes, Sister,' and fled. She flicked her hair back over her shoulder impatiently, wishing, not for the first time, that she could pluck up the resolve to get it cut. 'I'll pin up this mop as soon as I get old Ken under the shower,' she muttered to herself, just before grabbing the last free shower chair right under the nose of another rapidly approaching nurse.

The other nurse shrugged good-naturedly and grinned sympathetically but still with a hint of caution. Kaycee scowled as the girl disappeared and then shrugged. Oh, well, it was impossible to always live up to her reputation for being helpful and easy-going, she thought with a brief touch of humour, especially when she was feeling as though she should be in bed herself!

The patients allocated to her for the day greeted her cheerfully and then teased her mercilessly as they saw her dishevelled appearance, pale face and black-circled eyes. Mr Ken Rodgers was the worst. He had known her since she had toddled in with her mother and father the first time they had entered his grocery and hardware shop.

He chuckled at her gleefully. 'Been kickin' up ya heels at last, have ya, girl? 'Bout time! Must have been some eighteenth birthday party you put on last night for that brother of yours.'

Kaycee glared at her old friend. 'It went very well, thank you, Mr Rodgers,' she managed politely, and then snapped out, 'And I certainly have not been. . .not been kicking up my heels!'

Unfortunately!

The thought flashed through her mind. Why shouldn't she have been 'kicking up her heels'? Even if she had always had to be the sensible one, the practical one, of the family; even if she'd never had a serious relationship with a man, she was only twenty-six years old. Why should she have been the only one rushing around madly making sure that there was plenty of food and drink; making sure everyone was having a good time? Especially after. . .

She took a deep breath and forced her mind back to the task at hand. 'Now, Mr Rodgers, will you please let me get you onto this chair and out to the bathroom so you'll be finished before your breakfast arrives?'

The smile on the old man's face was replaced by a frown. 'No need to get uppity with me, young lady,' he wheezed, before allowing her to help him onto the chair.

Kaycee noted that this morning even that much exertion increased his breathlessness and remembered Jill's expressed concern that he had not slept very much. He had been admitted regularly over the years with bouts of chest infections. This was also not the first time that he had been admitted with pneumonia but this time he had taken much longer to respond to the antibiotics.

He coughed violently and she handed him his sputum container. Kaycee noted the small content when he had finished and frowned. She had not nursed him during his last couple of admissions so did not know if he was like this each time, but several times she had reported its scarcity and appearance. It was not like that usually caused by pneumonia or even bronchitis alone.

He mainly had these coughing spasms in the morning and what it produced was too little, too thick and viscous. She had seen it before and strongly suspected what it could be, especially with his history of increasingly severe chest infections.

She gave him a couple of moments to recover as she deliberately took her time collecting his toiletries and change of pyjamas. She handed them to him silently to hold so that she could grasp the chair handles.

'If it wasn't. . .the party. . .that's put that face on ya. . .then it was no doubt. . .ya mother,' the old man said jerkily between gasps.

Kaycee's hand clenched on the handles of the shower-chair. Had everyone else in the town, except her, realised what was going on? She had always detested the way gossip flew around this small town! Especially when everyone else knew what was happening in your own family before you knew yourself.

I want out, she thought savagely. And then she acknowledged with a slight sense of shock that it was a long time since she had really thought about her long-cherished dream of leaving Coolong. For many years she had told herself that once the mortgage was paid off and once Andrew had finished high school she would be able to get on with doing what she had wanted to ever since her father's fatal heart attack.

I want to go to a city where I can have some privacy, she thought with renewed determination. I hate this small town. I want to do what *I* want to for a change.

Fighting back the old hurt and anger of years, she kept her face averted and pushed on the shower-chair. Perhaps she was going too fast; perhaps she was temporarily blinded by the tears that she was trying desperately to prevent starting up all over again but Mr Rodgers gasped a warning a fraction too late. There was a bellow of pain as the steel footrests on the chair cannoned into someone in the corridor.

'Oh, my goodness!' she gasped with horror. Abandoning Mr Rodgers, she rushed to the assistance of the man who had stumbled back and was bent over rubbing his legs.

Pain and then outrage swamped Rowan Scott. This was all he needed!

Because of that wretched blocked fuel line, the car trip had taken well over twelve hours instead of eight. Then his host for the weekend, one of the partners in the only practice in Coolong, had left a message with his receptionist to tell him he'd had to rush off to Sydney because his father had suffered a coronary. Dr Taylor was very sorry but had asked the receptionist to book a room at a motel for the new doctor.

To make it all even crazier the worried-looking receptionist had handed him a long-range pager and nervously informed him that she was very sorry but he, the new locum, would have to take any calls until Monday when the third partner, Dr John Swain, would be back. He had also been called away unexpectedly only a few hours beforehand. The woman, who had merely introduced herself as 'I'm Sally', had mumbled something about 'family illness'.

Despite being more than a bit concerned at being the only doctor left in the town, Rowan had been so weary that he had not minded a quiet night by himself at all. The motel restaurant had provided a decent meal and the pager had remained silent but. . .

'For crying out loud, woman!' he bellowed. 'Why don't you look where you're going? As if a sleepless night wasn't enough I'm now attacked by a stupid. . .a stupid whoever you are!'

Straightening up to his full height, he glared down at the woman who had assaulted him. She looked like the one in the mauve uniform who had ignored him in the car park. He had shrugged and found his own way through the deserted reception area and eventually to a tiny staff-room near the casualty department. It, too, had been empty but at least there had been all the facilities to make himself some coffee and toast.

Now he stared at her. No wonder she had raced off!

His eyes travelled over a white face devoid of make-up. The dark brown eyes glaring at him were bloodshot and surrounded by dark smudges. In disbelief he gaped at the untidy, thick, dark brown hair that flowed across one shoulder and down over nicely rounded curves almost to her waist. The uniform looked as though it had been a long time since it had been touched by an iron.

'There. . .there usually isn't anyone else around at this time of the morning,' he heard her say in faltering tones.

He raised his eyes slowly to her face. Long, curling eyelashes flickered as she returned his stare, her own eyes filled with confusion and wariness.

What incredibly beautiful, expressive eyes, he thought in something of a daze. In fact, the whole package they came in was very beautiful despite the ravages of the night before. The unwelcome flair of awareness made him feel even more outraged.

'And that gives you the right to come charging out of a room like that?' he heard himself ask in a furious voice.

The nurse winced and then stiffened. One hand went up to rub the back of her neck. Instinctively he diagnosed a headache and a Saturday-night hangover! And what else would you expect of such a good-looking woman? Must have all the local yokels flocking around. . .

He took a deep breath and shook his head, his anger increasing with the trend of his wayward thoughts. Bending over, he hid his face for a moment and rubbed at his painful ankles again. He straightened and glared at her, determined to ignore the unwelcome frisson that those huge expressive eyes engendered.

As she stared back at him a variety of expressions flickered across her face. Then she blinked, lifted her chin and asked a little belligerently, 'Is the skin broken? Do you need some Betadine?'

He stood perfectly still, staring at her as though she was some creature from outer space. 'I know that life in a small country hospital is different but surely not this different,' he muttered.

He let his eyes blatantly study her crumpled uniform and untidy, dark brown hair again. She put out a well-shaped hand and flicked the heavy swathe of silk back over her shoulder self-consciously. A few more strands went flying loose from what he could now see was a haphazardly tied-back pony-tail. Bright red, glossy nail polish gleamed for a moment on well-shaped fingers before they disappeared into clenched fists.

His eyes quickly went back to her face and saw that a wave of red was sweeping into her cheeks. She bit her lip and avoided his eyes. Rowan suddenly realised that she was finding his blatant survey embarrassing and, if he was not mistaken, humiliating.

Then she tilted her chin higher and anger sparkled from her. 'If you don't need anything, I'm busy,' she snapped defensively. 'I'm running late already.' She paused and then swallowed rapidly, as though wishing she had not blurted out that piece of information. 'And if you're visiting someone you're too early,' she added ferociously.

'I think not.' His eyes went to her name badge. 'Unless of course, K. Wiseman EN, medical officers have to keep to visiting hours in your little hospital?'

K. Wiseman EN swallowed. The colour deepened on her face as her eyes widened in comprehension. Suddenly he found himself admiring the way she glared back at him, not giving an inch. Many far more mature women than this slip of a girl would have by this time been covered in confusion and abject apologies. Well, even a very small apology would be welcome if it took that angry, hating-all-doctors look off her exquisite face!

Suddenly his sense of humour started to surface for the first time since he had arrived in Coolong. The last twelve hours were certainly showing him how different these next few months would be. Having to be on call the moment he arrived and bawling cattle in the sale yards across the road from his motel had been warning enough, without this!

But, he decided suddenly with a glimmer of relief, this young woman's attitude was refreshingly different after the treatment most nurses had been handing out to him since he had split up with Sonja. This would have to be the most unusual welcome to his new life—away from the mad rush of Sydney—that he could ever have imagined! He felt the corners of his mouth twitch.

The nurse drew herself up. Her gaze swept over him, obviously mistaking his amusement at himself for laughter at her expense. Unexpected regret filled him as the brown eyes flashed disdain and dislike.

'Our little hospital expects all the doctors to visit

their *patients* whenever they should.' The words were sharp and the sarcasm unmistakable. She turned and grasped the handles of the chair again. The old man in it was staring curiously from one to the other. 'I think Sister Brooks is still in the office. Excuse me,' she added crisply, 'my patient's getting cold.'

He felt an inexplicable reluctance to let her go and his hand shot out to grab her arm. It was unexpectedly firm and quite cool. 'Just a moment, please. Where is the office?'

'At the end of this corridor turn right. You can't miss it,' she barked out and then, to his utter astonishment and fury, added nastily, 'Sister Brooks will be only too happy to croon over you!'

'Bit rude, weren't ya, Kaycee?' Mr Rodgers said with marked disapproval after the bathroom door had closed firmly behind them.

Kaycee had a horrible feeling that he was right. She had not only crashed into the big hot-shot doctor from the big hot-shot Sydney hospital but had behaved abominably! There had been a lot of speculation among the staff, as well as the townsfolk, about the locum coming to work at the one and only medical practice in Coolong and she, Kaycee Wiseman, had just taken out a lot of her own anger and upset on him.

He wasn't supposed to start until tomorrow. And how was I to know who he was, anyway? she excused herself feebly. Especially when your brain still isn't awake properly yet, girl.

But as she adjusted the shower water her hand shook. She was still tingling from the sense of disbelief that she had actually said what she had in the way she had and for no real reason she could now think of except that his whole attitude had rubbed her up the wrong way.

No, not just attitude, she seethed. It had been the way that his eyes had swept over her. The last sweep of his eyes had been filled with familiar masculine approval. That had made her feel uncomfortable enough without his obvious amazement at her dishevelled appearance. And he had dared to find her appearance amusing!

Right there and then she decided that she didn't like him, despite his beautifully tanned smooth skin and incredible bright blue eyes. To start with, she had never liked blond, tight curly hair on a man. Give her tall, dark and handsome any day!

Then she groaned inwardly, recalling how any amusement had been wiped out of those incredibly blue eyes and replaced by that startled expression of wrath as she had barrelled angrily past him. Her lateness and crumpled appearance would not be the only thing Sister would tell her off for today. And she would deserve every word!

But she was wrong. The young, second-year RN, who had not been at the hospital many months, never said a word to her. She was too full of the new, handsome young Doctor Rowan Scott. Her eyes even lit up when Kaycee informed her that Mr Sanders's IV site was swollen and the needle was obviously in the tissues now instead of the vein.

'I believe Dr Scott is fortunately still in the hospital, Kaycee,' Sister Brooks said with obvious satisfaction at having an excuse to call him to the ward again. 'He happened to be in the emergency department looking around when a scalded child came in.'

She paused and then added quickly, 'I know Mr

Sanders is your patient today but as you're running late
you don't have to stay with Dr Scott while he relocates
the drip. I'll show him where everything is.'

Kaycee was only too happy to have an excuse to
steer clear of those piercing eyes and leave him
to Bronwyn Brooks's tender ministrations. But at
morning tea there was to be no escape after all. A
slightly flushed RN ushered him into the small staff-
room to introduce him. And Bronwyn Brooks wasn't
the only one smitten, Kaycee realised as she watched
the reactions of her colleagues.

'And this is one of our enrolled nurses, Kaycee
Wiseman,' Sister Brooks beamed.

He surveyed her thoughtfully, inspecting Kaycee's
now neatly pinned-up hair and camouflage make-up.
Her hastily grabbed make-up bag had even yielded
nail-polish remover. A gleam entered his eyes. Kaycee
felt warmth flood her face. She had groaned out loud
when she had seen her wind-blown hair and untidy
appearance in a mirror shortly after their encounter.

The doctor's eyes fastened on her face. 'We've
already met, Sister Brooks.' He smiled. It was not a
particularly pleasant smile. Then he murmured, 'You
call her K-C as in the alphabet?'

Bronwyn Brooks gave a gay laugh. 'K-A-Y-C-E-E,'
she spelt out. 'Unusual isn't it? Sometimes we call
her Kay.'

Nothing infuriated Kaycee more than being talked
about as though she wasn't there. 'I prefer Kaycee,'
she said abruptly.

'Of course you do,' the man murmured. Then he
added gently, 'And you prefer the blues to crooning,
don't you, Kaycee?'

She stared at him in bewilderment for a moment,

and then anger flashed through her. She stood up. 'I don't sing at all. I prefer to listen to others make fools of themselves.'

A frown briefly creased his forehead. 'Hmm. . .' His voice deepened. 'If that is your attitude to beautiful music, beautifully sung, then I feel sorry for you, Kaycee—er—Wiseman, was it?' he asked very, very gently, and added in the same tones, 'Perhaps you should listen to some on Saturday nights instead of coming to work with a hangover on Sunday mornings.'

He turned abruptly to the RN beside him. She was looking with astonishment and increasing disapproval from Kaycee's now-furious, bright red face to the new doctor.

'Thank you for showing me around, Sister,' he said crisply. 'I hope I haven't held you up too much. I understand that I'm to be on call until tomorrow or until Dr Swain is able to return. But, if not before, I'll be in early tomorrow afternoon to do a full round of Dr Gordon's patients.' He ignored Kaycee's scarlet face, nodded to the others and disappeared.

No one moved for a moment. Then Sister Brooks said slowly, 'I suppose there was a reason for that confrontation, Nurse Wiseman?'

So he had not complained to her superior after all. The angry flush on Kaycee's cheeks faded, leaving her paler than before. She felt a sudden wave of exhaustion and nausea sweep over her.

'I'm. . .I'm afraid I collided with him in the corridor earlier, Sister,' she said wearily, and then felt herself sway and sat down again quickly.

'Are you feeling sick?' the sister asked abruptly.

Kaycee began automatically to shake her head and then paused. Her head was still throbbing and suddenly she felt drained and exhausted. She brushed a strand of hair away from her face. Why not? They weren't busy and she certainly felt sick enough every now and again. It would be the first time she had taken sick leave since that flu episode at least a couple of years ago.

And hopefully her mother would be up and about so that they could talk more about the shocking news the still-beautiful but hopelessly disorganised woman had flung at her midway through the previous evening.

'Yes, I do feel pretty dreadful. That gastric virus going around,' she added hastily as the RN's lips tightened.

'Oh, definitely; something going around!' The RN's voice oozed with sarcasm. Kaycee opened her mouth but she added abruptly. 'Finished your showers and beds?'

At Kaycee's quick nod, she said crisply, 'Report to Sister Allen. She's the hospital-in-charge RN this weekend. I think she's still in Emergency. Unfortunately, I doubt if she'll replace you now. It would have been better if you'd rung in sick to the night-in-charge supervisor. We'll have to finish the shift down a nurse. Perhaps you'd better take Dr Scott's advice another time.'

That was too much! Kaycee rose. 'His diagnosis was very wrong. I didn't feel at all well before my brother's birthday party. I do not have a hangover,' she snapped. 'I've never had a hangover in my life!'

Kaycee stormed off to find the supervisor, ignoring the increasing anger in the sister's face. No doubt she would hear this about that piece of impertinence as well at some future date!

And I hope I never do have a hangover if it feels like this, Kaycee thought wearily a little later as she

collected her things and left the ward. She refused to
feel sorry that the staff would no longer be able to have
a relaxing shift with her work to do as well as their
own. After all, there had been many times over the
years when she had been left to do someone else's
work on a shift.

She felt more upset knowing that she had offended
the new doctor. He would be in and out of the hospital
a lot during the next three months of his time in
Coolong and could make life very difficult for her if
he wanted to.

As she made her way through the hospital to the car
park, Kaycee thought about that. At least he had not
told Sister how she had sniped at him. Then she thought
of the cold expression in those darkened blue eyes
and the warning she had not mistaken despite it being
delivered in such gentle tones.

She shivered and it wasn't only from the cold westerly wind that swept across the car park. Somehow she
knew that she would have to apologise and perhaps tell
him that she was known more for her kindness and
sympathy than her sharp tongue.

Kaycee had almost reached her car when she noticed
the tall figure standing near the racy-looking red car.
She stood still and took a deep breath.

So he was the man she had glimpsed so briefly in
the car park and ignored. He was standing with his
back towards her, staring out across the grassy hillside
sloping away from the hospital to the range of mountains that ringed the small country town towards the
west. There was no mistaking the blond curls being
lifted by the strong breeze. His hands were in his coat
pockets, his shoulders a little hunched and rounded.

There was something rather lonely about that tall man standing so motionless.

She started unlocking her car but then stopped. Perhaps she should get that apology over with now. She hesitated a moment longer and, when the solitary figure still did not stir, started towards him.

Gravel crunched under Kaycee's foot and the doctor swung sharply around. There was such a forbidding expression on his face that Kaycee paused several feet away, suddenly wishing that she had left him alone.

Then recognition swept into his eyes. As his sharp gaze swept over her he suddenly scowled ferociously.

Kaycee almost changed her mind. But there had been numerous challenges during the past eight years that she'd had to cope with by herself so she took a deep breath and took another step closer, her eyes glued to his face. She opened her mouth to speak and somehow it stayed open as he gave an irritable gesture and swore suddenly and violently before striding angrily forward and grasping her arm.

'You stupid girl! Don't you have any sense at all?' he bellowed at her.

Almost before she knew it he had pulled her over to the low, red sports car and bundled her inside, slamming the door on her protesting squeak.

CHAPTER TWO

ROWAN stormed around the car and fumbled with cold fingers to open his door. By the time he had settled into his seat and turned to this annoying young woman, she was staring at him nervously and already fumbling for her doorhandle. He couldn't blame her. She must think she had been manhandled by a lunatic! He could have at least done his knight-in-shining-armour bit with a lot more finesse.

Standing there in the freezing westerly wind he had been feeling thoroughly disgusted with himself at the way he had spoken to a nurse in front of her colleagues. There had been something about the woman that had flung out a challenge to him, to which he had stupidly responded with petty sarcasm and reprimand. He had almost decided to go back and apologise when he had swung around and there she was. He couldn't believe that she wasn't even wearing a lightweight cardigan in this cold wind.

Reaching over to the back seat he grabbed a travelling rug. Ignoring her startled protest, he tucked it around her.

'It's bad enough feeling guilty for getting you into trouble with your sister. I don't want to add getting pneumonia to the list,' he growled as he finished pulling it up around her shoulders so that her arms were trapped and only her startled face was still visible.

A tantalising, delicate perfume reached him. He flung himself back in his seat away from a sudden

22

desire to reach out and touch the satin sheen of her cheeks. Instead he snarled, 'Only an idiot would be wearing a short-sleeved cotton uniform in this cold wind. What are you doing out here without even a cardigan?'

Great Scott! So much for apologising! Now the woman will be convinced you're a moron.

Kaycee could not remember the last time someone had thought she needed taking care of. Warmth that was not just from the covering of the blanket flooded through her as she gaped at him.

'I. . .I was running late and forgot. . .' she stammered weakly, mesmerised by the mixture of anger and concern in the face staring intently back at her.

With an effort she pulled herself together and started to push her arms free of the rug. He started to protest and she added sharply, 'It's not that darned cold anyway!'

'That wind's freezing!'

He certainly looked chilled. Pulling his coat closer around himself and crossing his arms he tucked his hands under his armpits. He shivered and suddenly looked like her brother had as a small boy years ago on cold winter mornings.

Unexpectedly a bubble of laughter started up deep inside Kaycee and she grinned. 'It's not that bad when you've lived here for a while. Especially after a few seasons of the westerlies blowing off heavy falls of snow on the Barrington Tops. Today's quite mild in comparison. Besides, I'll have you know this is a beautiful, sunny spring day.'

His gaze intensified, sweeping over her features with an expression that was far from hostile. With an inward sigh of relief she relaxed still more. Obviously he was not the type of man who resented being laughed at.

He gave a mock shudder. 'I knew I should have delayed leaving Brisbane until the summer.'

Her eyes widened. 'Brisbane? I thought you'd been working in Sydney.'

A gleam flashed into his eyes. They really were an incredible blue, Kaycee thought a little helplessly. Like a deep tropical sea. Then she remembered the sternness in them as he had subtly told her off in front of the staff. This was definitely not a man to relax too much around. Kaycee sat up a little straighter.

'Aha! The hospital grapevine works even here, I see,' he drawled sarcastically. 'That's right, I have been working in Sydney but have just returned from an extended holiday in sunny Brisbane.'

'The hospital grapevine? Make that the town grapevine!' Kaycee heard the bitterness creep into her voice. 'I actually heard in the supermarket about your coming from Sydney.'

He looked at her silently for a moment. 'Sounds like you don't like the town,' he murmured at last.

'Oh, most people seem to think Coolong's all right, I suppose.' Kaycee shrugged slightly and then her voice hardened. 'I just hate small towns, full stop. Everybody knows everybody else's business before they even know themselves. And gossip can do tremendous damage. Especially. . .especially. . .'

She broke off. Deliberately she pushed the past back deep into her mind where it had not been allowed to surface for so many years.

As a faint gleam of speculation entered those brilliant eyes, Kaycee wished fervently once again that she'd kept her mouth shut. What was it about this man that made her blurt out the first thing that came into her mind?

To her relief and surprise, his face slowly lit up. 'Ah, I'm a victim of small-town gossip already.'

There was such a wealth of satisfaction in his voice that Kaycee stared. 'You actually sound pleased about that!'

He grinned at her. Suddenly his face looked much younger, more carefree. 'It sure beats the impersonal nature of the big city I've been living in the past few years.' He sobered quickly then and a bleak look crossed his face just before he turned his head away.

'Well, I hate small towns and this one especially.'

Kaycee knew that she sounded angry and fed up. An extra jab of pain shot through her head. She winced and closed her eyes, one hand reaching up to rub at her scalp. What on earth was she doing discussing the virtues and problems of living in a town like Coolong when she was on her way home to collapse?

'Why did you come chasing after me in the middle of your shift?' The male voice sounded irritable again.

Kaycee's eyes flew open to see him scowling once again at her.

'I wouldn't have bawled you out next time I saw you if you hadn't apologised by then.'

Kaycee stared blankly at him for a moment. The arrogance of the man!

Quickly she tossed the rug aside. 'I did not come chasing after you to apologise! Well. . .er. . .not at first, anyway,' she corrected hurriedly, remembering that she had approached him with that very intention. 'I'm on my way home,' she finished sharply. 'I don't feel very well.'

'Hangovers have a nasty habit of making you feel like that.'

Amusement had softened his voice but Kaycee flared, 'I have not got a hangover!'

His eyes narrowed. 'One of your patients and an old friend, I understand, thought otherwise. I think he said his name was Mr Rodgers. The one in the shower-chair,' he added with a faint smile. 'Apparently you had a family party last night.'

'He's mistaken.' Kaycee turned her face away. 'Oh, we had my brother's birthday party but we didn't serve any alcohol,' she told him wearily, not adding that because of the argument about that with her mother she had come close to wiping her hands of the responsibility she had felt towards the under-age teenagers she knew would be at the party.

She looked for the doorhandle again, and opened the door slightly. 'I just didn't get much sleep. Something happened that. . .that. . .' She stopped abruptly and then glanced briefly at him again. 'Look, I'm taking the rest of the day off. I do feel pretty ghastly.'

A large tanned hand reached across and gently turned her face towards him. He studied her for a moment. 'How were you going to get home?'

All amusement had disappeared from his searching eyes. She stared back at him, suddenly feeling very unsure of herself—something her family would never have believed. Sympathetic understanding filled his face and warmth again rocketed through her. Then his large hand turned. The coolness of the back of his index finger against her suddenly warm cheek made her jerk away.

'That. . .that's my car—the little yellow one.' She nodded a little breathlessly and then winced again as the sudden movement of her head sent a shooting pain through it.

'You aren't well enough to drive,' he said decisively. 'I'll take you home. Do shut the door and close the cold wind out,' he added sharply.

That strange warm glow intensified. Kaycee knew she should be annoyed at his bossy manner but she found herself rather enjoying his concern for her. After searching his face a moment longer she closed the door.

'That's very kind of you,' she murmured a little unsteadily, 'but there's really no need. Besides, I live a little out of town.'

'That would be all of five minutes away, I suppose?'

'At least fifteen. . .' Kaycee began and then realised his eyes were smiling again. She stopped uncertainly.

'Only a hop, skip and a jump in the big smoke.' He leaned forward and started the engine and the smile reached his well-shaped mouth.

'Besides, my sister brought me up to be a gentleman. Come on, tell me which way to go. I was delayed and only arrived after dark last night. Haven't seen much of Coolong except from the surgery to the motel and then to the hospital this morning. And a certain cattle sale yard,' he added rather grimly. 'You can point out a few things on the way.'

Kaycee hesitated for only a few more moments. She was really feeling wretched and this car was far more comfortable than her old bomb, especially since the car heater had stopped working a few days ago. Her brother could drive over with one of his friends who had stayed the night and pick it up. After all that she had done for him in the last few days it was the least he could do.

She reached for her seat belt decisively. 'Thank you, that's very kind of you.'

He just grinned back at her, his whole face lighting up this time, and then turned his attention to putting the car into motion. Something kindled deep within Kaycee. A little confused at the unexpected feeling, she quickly gave him directions and soon they were driving down the slope towards the main shopping centre.

He fired a few questions at her about the town. Kaycee answered them briefly, telling him about the town's facilities. Before she knew it she had relaxed at his easy manner and soon found herself pointing out the post office and her favourite supermarket of the two the town boasted.

As they drove past the large high school she told him, 'Nearly five hundred students go there now. Besides Coolong, students are picked up by bus from outlying smaller communities. Only just over two thousand people actually live in Coolong but more than double that number live in the area. The school has a great choice of subjects. Andrew, my brother, finished his Year Twelve there last year.'

She paused and then added proudly, 'His tertiary level made it possible to start his training this year at Newcastle University to be a doctor.'

'Poor devil,' Doctor Scott said unexpectedly. He caught her look of surprise and added quickly, 'I still have very vivid memories of my first-year medical training in Sydney. Is he the brother who's just celebrated his birthday?'

'Yes, his eighteenth.'

'A bit young to be halfway through his first year, isn't he?'

Kaycee hesitated and then asked anxiously. 'Do you think so? I thought he was, too, at the beginning of the year and tried to persuade him to defer and get a job this year. But it was so hard to get anything with the unemployment so bad and. . .' She bit her lip, suddenly realising that she was sharing one of her own deep feelings of concern about her family scene to a stranger.

'Anyway,' she added brightly, 'he seems to have grown up a lot his first semester. Hasn't got all his assignment results but he thinks he's done OK. Oh, turn left here, please.'

As long as Kaycee could remember she had lived in the sprawling old family home on a small acreage near the outskirts of the town.

In the earlier years they had kept ponies, fowls, rabbits and even guinea pigs. But always there had been the natural bush beyond their land, running down to the little creek. It had been a wonderful place to play games like pirates and hidden treasures or merely to stroll beside the slowly trickling water in the early morning or evening, hoping to see an elusive platypus.

A very young Andrew had once claimed to see one of the small furry mammals with the big bills but as no one else ever had, she had thought it had probably been the product of a wishful, inventive young mind.

Their mother had always worried about being so close to the bush because of the ever-present fear of bush fires. So they had always kept the grass cut and made sure that no gum-tree saplings were allowed to grow close to the house.

During the last few years more land in the vicinity had been subdivided into house blocks and the town had crept closer—something that had saddened Kaycee but delighted her mother. As the demand for land increased no doubt the value of their property had also, Kaycee thought with a touch of bitterness.

A few minutes later the red car turned onto the rough, gravelled track that led to the house that was set well back from the road. There had been no money to have the road repaired for a long time, or so her mother had insisted. Another hint that Kaycee had missed? Had she considered it a wasted expense which would not have necessarily increased the property's value?

As the wheels hit a pothole, the low-slung car was scraped underneath. It jolted Kaycee's attention back to her companion.

'Oh, I'm sorry, I should have warned you it was so rough.'

'My fault,' Rowan Scott said cheerfully. 'I was too busy looking at that large marquee. Did you put that up just for the party?'

There was considerable surprise in his deep voice and Kaycee's expression hardened. 'Yes, Mum's friend insisted on hiring it for us,' she said abruptly. And Bob Gould had better pay for it, she thought fiercely for the hundredth time. I certainly don't have any money for it.

Since her mother had added him to her list of the boyfriends she had acquired over the years since her husband had died, he had been intruding more and more into their family life. He had certainly lasted the longest—almost twelve months.

Bob had always been pleasant enough to Kaycee but she had never bothered to spend any more time in his presence than common courtesy had dictated. Now she felt a little guilty about resenting him as much as she did. Last night he had turned out to be a capable MC at the party. Come to think of it, he had been very supportive in several ways.

She bit her bottom lip. But had it been his influence

that had caused her mother to make her decision? What was behind it all?

Kaycee saw Rowan glance at her averted face briefly but he was silent until he had parked the car. Then, as he opened his door, he ordered in a firm voice, 'Keep that rug around you.'

She stiffened at his bossy tone but he had already disappeared and she felt too miserable anyway to protest. By the time she joined him he was looking appreciatively at the large brick house with its wide verandas set against the backdrop of towering gum-trees.

'This is very beautiful.' His voice was filled with pleasure. 'Have you always lived here, Kaycee?'

Kaycee swallowed on the sudden, unexpected lump in her throat. Never until last night had she realised how much she loved her home. Always before it had seemed like an unnecessary drain on their finances—an added burden that had kept her from doing what she wanted to away from Coolong.

'It. . .it's the only home I remember,' she muttered, and then said in a firmer voice as she joined him, 'My dad bought it not long after we moved here. I was only two.'

A sudden loud blast of a combination of electric guitars and drums came from the marquee.

'Oh, no,' Kaycee groaned, one hand massaging her temple. 'I hoped they might still all be asleep or gone out somewhere!'

Rowan looked startled and then gave a chuckle. 'A sleep-over party, was it?'

'Very much so,' Kaycee said grimly, 'only there was very little sleep.' She took a couple of steps towards the abominable noise and then paused. 'Would you like to come and meet my brother and his friends?' she offered impulsively and then flushed and rushed to add, 'Or would you prefer to go straight up to the house for a hot drink? Or perhaps—'

'I'd love to meet a budding med student,' Rowan interrupted her gently.

By the time they reached the entrance to the marquee the noise was deafening. On the rough wooden platform at the far end a couple of guitars were being played with more noise and enthusiasm than musical ability. The slight figure behind the set of drums was pounding them energetically.

Kaycee strode rapidly across the marquee and flicked a couple of switches. The guitars cut off. The musicians looked up and called out indignantly.

'Pack them away, boys,' Kaycee said firmly. She looked around at the mess of scattered chairs, trestle tables and drooping decorations. Air mattresses and sleeping bags were still scattered around the bare wooden platform. She put her hands on her hips. 'And I thought you were going to have this all cleared away by now, including the electric extension cables. It's a wonder the hire firm haven't arrived already to start dismantling the marquee.'

'Ah, Kaycee!' the drummer said angrily. He gave one more loud drum roll and then stood up. 'We've been working on a new idea.'

'Then you'll have to work on it somewhere else, Drew,' she told him crisply. 'And not in the house, either. I've got a headache.'

Kaycee sighed inwardly as the tall, thin teenager strode rapidly towards them. Why on earth had her brother decided to wear his oldest, scruffiest pair of jeans and ragged jumper this morning of all mornings?

University uniform, she had thought several times, as most of his fellow students dressed so similarly. And then she wondered suddenly why it mattered so much what Rowan Scott thought of her family.

'Dr Scott, this is my brother, Andrew,' she hastened to introduce them as the teenager raised his eyebrows enquiringly.

'Call me Rowan, please,' the doctor said firmly as he shook Drew's hand. 'I believe you're a first-year med student. How are you enjoying it?'

Drew's smile was a little lopsided. 'Some bits are OK; others I'm not too sure about yet. Are you the locum for old Doc Gordon?'

Rowan Scott nodded with a smile. Before he could answer Kaycee said rapidly, 'Drew, would you mind looking after Dr Scott while I lie down for a while?'

Concern flashed across her brother's face. He glanced at her uniform. 'That's right, you had to work this morning because that other nurse could not swap a shift. Why you don't stick up for yourself, I'm blowed if I know,' he burst out irritably with a scowl. 'What are you doing home now?'

'To recover from your party,' Rowan Scott said a little sharply.

Kaycee looked at him indignantly. 'I told you, I do not have a hangover!'

Drew gave a high hoot of laughter. 'Kaycee with a hangover? That'll be the day!'

Kaycee glared at him. Did he have to make her sound so boring in front of Rowan?

'I wish you could say the same thing,' she said through gritted teeth and then felt a flash of shame as red tinged her brother's cheeks.

'There's no need to bring up that one unfortunate

episode last year,' Drew snarled so savagely that her
eyes widened in disbelief.

It was so unlike her usually sunny-tempered, adoring
brother that she felt a strong twinge of unease. It had
not been the first time this weekend that he had seemed
different. But, then, who knew what pressures he'd had
this past week?

She bit back on her natural retort and said quietly
instead, 'You're right. Sorry, Drew.' She forced a brief
smile for forgiveness before turning to Dr Scott. He
was watching her brother with a slight frown. 'Thank
you very much for the lift home. Would you mind if I
left you to Drew to look after?'

'Not at all,' Rowan said sympathetically. 'I'll no
doubt see you tomorrow at the hospital.'

Thoughtfully Rowan watched her as she walked
slowly away, at last disappearing around the side of
the tent. 'I wonder if I should have offered her some
medication,' he muttered out loud.

'Kaycee? No way.' Her brother shrugged as Rowan
raised an eyebrow at him. 'She's got a very well-
stocked medicine cupboard. Besides, doubt if she'd
take anything, anyway,' he added with unconcern as
he turned back to one of his friends. 'She's never sick.'

Rowan looked at him thoughtfully after he had been
introduced and shaken hands with the guitar players.
When first-year med students looked so young to him
he must be getting old!

'OK, you guys, better do what big sis said and get
this place cleaned up,' Andrew said firmly.

Despite the chorus of groans, it was obvious that
'big sis' was to be obeyed and they started packing
away the instruments and sound system with a will.
They accepted Rowan's offer of help only too gladly,

chatting away to him about the 'beaut' party the night before.

Rowan put his thoughts into words as he brought over a couple of chairs to add to a stack. 'It was good of your mother and father to organise such a big do for you, Andrew.'

'My dad died about nine years ago,' Andrew answered quietly. 'He and Dr Gordon started that practice you're working for,' he added proudly.

Rowan glanced at him swiftly. Nine years. That had been how long Kaycee had told him she had been a nurse. And being a nurse for so long was not the only reason she had not been at all self-conscious with a doctor like himself. She had grown up knowing one intimately. His lips twisted in self-mockery. Kaycee didn't need any more reason to treat him other than she had than her own personality!

'There's only Mum and my two sisters. Unfortunately, Jan lives in Canberra and is close to having her first baby. Mum's in a real flap about that.' Andrew laughed boisterously. 'My dear mum's hopeless at anything like this at the best of times. Kaycee always organises things.'

'Then you're very fortunate to have a sister like her,' Rowan responded. More than fortunate, he thought as he looked around at the evidence of the hard work that she must have put into it. 'No wonder she was so exhausted this morning.'

Andrew scowled. 'It all rather got out of hand,' he snapped angrily. 'I only discovered that when I arrived home a couple of days ago. Mum's boyfriend had ordered this marquee, which was just as well as it turned out. Apparently Mum had invited a lot of her friends and forgotten to add them to Kaycee's list until yesterday.'

Not only extra space would have been needed, Rowan thought a little grimly. There would have been extra food and drinks to organise. No wonder she had been so exhausted!

The sound of a car slowly negotiating the rough entrance reached them.

'That'll be Mum now.' Andrew shrugged. 'You'd better come and be introduced.' He hesitated and then said slowly, 'I know she'll be glad to meet the new doctor at Dad's old practice.' He hesitated as though to add something further and then shrugged irritably as a car door slammed.

The woman who rushed into the tent looked worried and frazzled. She started talking the minute she reached the entrance. 'Oh, Drew, haven't you finished in here yet? Bob was so sorry he couldn't stay to help. Kaycee will be so cross if we haven't finished before—' She broke off and stared at the stranger. 'Hello, who are you? Oh, dear, I'm afraid there's no time now to entertain anyone. . .'

'Mum!' roared Andrew.

Her mouth closed with a snap and she stared at Andrew.

Rowan frowned. The boy's hands were clenched, his whole body tight with tension. He was breathing a little faster and then he swallowed a couple of times before smiling faintly at his mother and shrugging.

'Look, Mum, I'm sorry,' he said in an obviously carefully controlled voice. 'Everything's under control. Come and meet Doctor Scott. He—'

'Doctor! What's happened? Is it Kaycee? Has she been hurt?'

The fear, almost panic, in Mrs Wiseman's voice swung Rowan's attention from Andrew. She hurried to a stop and stared anxiously up at him.

'No, no,' Andrew said hurriedly. 'Rowan is just helping us. He brought Kaycee home—'

'Home! But she should still be at work! Is she all right?'

'I should imagine Kaycee will be fine after she's had a good sleep, Mrs Wiseman,' Rowan said briskly. 'She developed a very bad headache and they let her come home.'

'Oh dear, oh dear. . .I *told* her it was too much for her to do all that cooking, especially when she had to work yesterday morning! We could have *bought* more food! Bob told her he'd help!'

'Mum, you know Kaycee; she never listens to either of us.' Andrew's voice was sharp. Once again he made a visible effort at self-control. He put an arm around his mother and began to lead her towards the house. 'Look, you must be worn out, too. It was a shame Bob's car wouldn't start this morning and you had to run him all the way home. Why don't you go and have a rest while we finish up here?'

He winked over his shoulder at Rowan and kept urging his protesting parent towards the house.

Rowan watched them for a moment before turning away to continue packing up. It was very obvious that both brother and sister seemed to be more the parent than the mother. And Bob must be the boyfriend. From his tone Andrew held no animosity towards him although by the resentment in Kaycee's voice she certainly did.

A frown creased Rowan's forehead. As she had turned to go into the house there had been great despondency, as well as weariness, in Kaycee. Suddenly he suspected that her exhaustion was from far more than the last few hectic days. Was there that weariness of the soul after years of being the mainstay, the strength of her family for far too long?

His hands clenched on the chair he had picked up. It landed with unnecessary force on the stack of chairs. She reminded him too much of his own sister—of the way she had struggled for so many years to be the provider and strength of their family.

Well, once he had only wanted to escape from Elle and a country town. He had succeeded. Sydney had been exciting. He had made lots of friends. There had been the hectic years through university.

At first he had really enjoyed the challenge of working at the large city hospital. Then the last couple of years he had begun to wonder if the impersonal heart of the big city with its noise, the rush and bustle, was where he wanted to live and work for the rest of his life. The need to escape back to the country, even for a short period, had grown stronger.

But there had not only been the great opportunities for promotion at that hospital; there had been other entanglements in his personal life, Sonja being the main one. The girl he had thought he knew and grown to believe he would one day marry.

Andrew re-entered the marquee and Rowan deliberately tried to block off the memory of the last frustrating months. The teenager rather listlessly recommended tidying the marquee. Rowan unobtrusively watched him for a moment. The late night had certainly taken a toll on him, as well as his sister, but then he frowned. The young man still seemed angry as he flashed a forced smile at Rowan but his movements were slow.

Too lethargic for someone who still seemed angry.

Problems, his doctor's instinct diagnosed. Then he paused. And not only this boy. The relationship between his mother and sister apparently had something lacking. Almost reluctantly he let his mind at last dwell on that exhausted, yet still beautiful and strangely appealing woman with eyes that flashed fire.

He acknowledged to himself at last that there was something about her that had touched a place deep inside him that not even Sonja had been allowed to penetrate.

He clanged another chair onto a stack. He had not come here to Coolong to become involved with any woman. Especially a woman with family problems. Even more, especially a woman who so obviously disliked the small country town living that he had set his heart on!

Andrew yelled across at one of his friends. Rowan paused and looked sharply at them. Suddenly he was silently laughing at himself. 'Who are you kidding, Rowan Scott?' he murmured under his breath. 'You're already involved with this family whether you like it or not!'

CHAPTER THREE

IT WAS a burst of male laughter that woke Kaycee. A couple of paracetamol tablets had at last eased the pounding in her head and she had fallen into an exhausted sleep. She sat up slowly, for a brief moment wishing that she could just stay there. But no doubt there would still be a mess to finish cleaning up in the kitchen, despite her efforts until well after midnight.

The bedroom was cold and she threw on her old warm dressing gown. She frowned as she made her way down the corridor. Surely Andrew and his friends had not missed their bus back to Newcastle.

The first thing she saw as she entered the warm kitchen was Rowan Scott's handsome face as he threw back his head and laughed loudly again at something her mother had just said. He was sitting at the table with a mug in his hands and a selection of leftover goodies from the party in front of him.

Kaycee's mother, looking slim and pampered in her expensive new track suit, was flushed and beaming down at him. She stood at the kitchen sink actually doing something as mundane as peeling a potato. When she saw Kaycee in the doorway her smile faltered and then disappeared.

'So there you are, Kaycee, and about time too,' Mrs Wiseman said disapprovingly. 'Sleeping half the day away means you won't be able to sleep tonight.'

She turned back to Rowan Scott and beamed at him again. 'I believe this kind young man had to drive you

home this morning. So good of him.' Then she added
a little too quickly, 'And guess what, Kaycee? There's
been a real mix-up arranging his accommodation. He
hasn't been able to find a place to stay yet, except at
that ghastly motel next to the sale yards. Even that
special room at the hospital is already occupied by
someone or other. So he's going to board here with us!'

Kaycee's eyes flew to Rowan. He was watching her
over the brim of his cup. As he carefully put it back
onto the saucer he steadily held her gaze, his face
expressionless.

Kaycee closed her eyes for a moment and then said
indignantly, 'Mother, what about. . .?' She paused and
swallowed. She glanced again at Rowan and then
swiftly away from his narrowed gaze. 'What about
those plans of yours to. . .to sell the house?'

Kaycee swallowed again on the hard knot of bewilderment and sense of betrayal. For years her mother
had left all the difficult financial decisions to her. And
now. . .

How could her mother have made the important
decision to sell their home without giving her a hint
that she was thinking of it, let alone talk it over with
her first?

Mrs Wiseman looked uncertain for a moment. Then
she turned away and grabbed another potato, tossing
over her shoulder, 'Now, don't go on about that again!
My mind's made up and that's final!'

The deep hurt and anger that had swamped Kaycee
last night at the party and then kept her awake began
to rise up again. She took a deep breath, holding onto
her self-control with an effort.

'If that's the case then don't you think it's rather

pointless Dr Scott coming to live here for such a brief time?'

Mrs Wiseman's shoulders tensed and then slumped. She turned slowly around, eyes wide with consternation. 'Oh, dear,' she said helplessly. Then she brightened again.

'But it could take months to find a buyer and then weeks to exchange contracts. Rowan has already booked out of the motel and has his things here already. I told him we had a spare room. I was going to clear it out but when he saw all your old stuff in there he refused to. . .to. . .' She stopped uncertainly as she saw the expression on her daughter's face.

'Mother! How dare you. . .!' Kaycee began furiously and then paused, speechless with anger and deep hurt. Her mother had actually taken a stranger to intrude on a part of her life that she had always kept very private!

Rowan Scott stood up abruptly. 'I knew you would prefer to move your things yourself, Kaycee. Besides, I haven't actually said I had accepted your kind offer, Mrs Wiseman, and my things are in my car because I had to book out of the motel this morning before ten. I said I thought Kaycee should be consulted first.'

There was a hint of steel behind the quiet words. He moved forward and put a large hand on Kaycee's arm. 'However, I quite understand if it's not convenient, after all. Leave your mother to finish putting that casserole in the oven she was preparing for tea while we have a talk about it.'

Kaycee glanced sharply from him back to her mother. Until recently her mother had rarely stirred herself to prepare meals, especially the main evening one. Even all the cooking for the party had been done by herself as usual. Her mother had stated firmly that she would only wear herself out if she helped.

She glanced around the kitchen. Wonder of wonders, there wasn't a thing out of place. Someone had certainly been busy in here. A slight flush touched her mother's cheeks and she tilted her chin as Kaycee looked at her.

Kaycee hesitated for a brief moment and then decided to ignore the warning flags of indignation starting to appear on her mother's face. 'That's a very good idea,' she said abruptly, and turned on her heel and left the room too fast for her mother to voice any protest.

Knowing that Rowan was close behind her, she went through to the wide veranda and paused to stare blindly out across the garden.

'I'm sorry, Kaycee.' Behind her, Rowan's voice was filled with regret.

Kaycee, avoiding his glance, fought to control the anger and old pain that surfaced so often in encounters with her mother. Then she felt him take her hand as he moved in front of her. A finger tilted her chin up so that she could no longer avoid his eyes.

'As soon as I saw the things in that room I knew I was intruding. I assure you I only stood in the doorway for a brief moment,' he added hurriedly as Kaycee felt embarrassed colour creep into her face again.

'I. . .I don't really mind,' she said huskily. 'It's just that Mum has never understood or. . .or liked me shutting myself away in there by myself. I used to do them—my projects—in my bedroom before my sister married. We rarely use her old room now so I decided to spread my things out in there. That way I don't have to pack them up all the time.' She realised that she was starting to babble and broke off, forcing a weak smile.

'My sister was very artistic.' Rowan's smile was

filled with gentle understanding. 'She didn't like strangers seeing her efforts before she had finished them.'

A tender light filled Rowan's eyes and suddenly Kaycee knew that it was all right that this man might have seen her attempts at painting landscapes and portraits—even folk art on polished wooden frames and boxes of all shapes and sizes. Her latest efforts she was particularly sensitive about. She had been experimenting with collages; decorating old wooden chairs for ornaments—even one with a setting for a lamp.

'I thought it also looked like it might be your escape hole,' Rowan added softly.

And Kaycee suddenly knew that he was right. Without her realising it on a conscious level, her arts and crafts work had become her escape from the responsibilities that had at times seemed too much. Since Bob Gould had become almost a daily visitor the last few weeks she had spent almost all her spare time at home in there, even if that spare time had been in even shorter supply lately than it ever had.

Rowan felt a wave of tenderness as Kaycee avoided his eyes and nervously tightened the belt of her dressing gown. Her hair was as long as he had known it would be. It fell in a ruffled, gleaming curtain around her and made her look young and vulnerable—so different from the bedraggled nurse who had confronted him so belligerently early that morning.

Suddenly she flung aside her hair and looked up at him. The puzzled, uncertain look on her face made his heart quicken.

His eyes travelled over her still far too pale, beautifully shaped features. Her lips were moist and full and his eyes lingered before following her slender throat down to the soft swell at the deep V of her dressing gown.

His gaze returned to her lips and he watched, fascinated, as her tongue nervously moistened them. Then white teeth gripped the bottom lip and his eyes flew up and then quickly away again.

Her dark brown eyes had darkened with confusion and. . .and embarrassment!

He raked his hand through his hair impatiently, annoyed with himself. A state he seemed to be constantly in around this woman! But, all the same, she had been examining him as closely as he had her beautiful features and body. The atmosphere between them had subtly changed. His eyes dropped once again to her lips.

He swallowed.

Then he was staring into her eyes again. Something crept into them. A flare of awareness. . .curiosity. . .

Her eyelids drooped. His heart leapt. She, too, was wondering what it would be like to feel his lips on hers. A tide of red swept into her cheeks and she looked quickly away.

Sudden heat rushed through him. His hands started to reach for her. Then he froze. Careful, Scott, he sternly reminded himself. No entanglements. Especially with one of the nurses!

Kaycee blindly stared in front of her. For one crazy moment she had wanted to feel that beautifully moulded mouth on hers. She had wanted to reach out and touch that lean brown throat.

The huge tent caught her eye. Abruptly she moved towards the steps. 'Oh, they haven't come for the marquee yet,' she exclaimed with a feeling of relief at having an excuse to change the subject. Hopefully, if she put a little distance between them that strange tension that had developed would disappear.

There was a stillness behind her and she suddenly held her breath.

It's too soon, she thought frantically. Far too soon! We only met a few hours ago.

Then she sensed him move and she released her breath on a deep sigh of relief.

'It's OK. Drew and his mates have cleared everything away.' Rowan's voice was a little harsh and held a trace of impatience. 'I believe the hire firm rang to say they were delayed or something.'

Kaycee felt his hand on her arm. She stiffened.

Abruptly the hand was removed. 'Look, Kaycee, about boarding here. Obviously it's not convenient so I'll just see if I can have that room at the motel for a few nights. I'll visit a real estate agent first thing tomorrow—even today if one happens to be open. If necessary, the motel will do until something comes up. Hopefully Coolong doesn't have a cattle sale every Monday!'

Kaycee felt an unexpected regret. It would have been rather nice to have the opportunity to spend more time with this sensitive, handsome man. She turned to him impulsively.

'Oh, Rowan, I'm so sorry. I guess you had as little sleep last night as I did. Look, Coolong always has very few places for rent. Mum knows that. It'll be no big deal moving my things. It's just Mum's attitude that gets under my skin. You're more than welcome to stay here but you might only be here a short while and still have to move.

'You see, I. . . That is, Mum. . .Mum has already put the house up for sale. She only told me last night.' She swallowed hard. Putting it into words made it all so horribly real.

'And does her having hit you with that information have something to do with your hangover that wasn't a hangover?' she heard the quiet voice ask softly.

His eyes were very kind, his expression sympathetic. Kaycee studied him for a moment. Then he reached out and tucked her hands into his strong ones. This time she didn't move. Suddenly it didn't seem at all strange to let him touch her. It was there again. That warm feeling of being cared for. Being looked after.

If his long arms closed about her she would be able to lean on him and he would never let her down.

Ridiculous. She'd only met him this morning. She didn't even know the man!

'You must have a very good bedside manner,' she said huskily.

His expression lightened. His hand tightened on hers and then his eyes twinkled devilishly. 'So I've been told before,' he murmured.

Kaycee felt the colour flood her face. She snatched her hands away and glared at him.

'Oops!' Grinning openly, he shook his head at her. His rejected hands rested on his slim hips. 'Just wrecked that bedside manner. I'll have to practise some more.' There was a loud clatter from the direction of the kitchen. He grabbed Kaycee's hand again. 'Let's go for a drive. You can show me more of Coolong.'

'But I can't go like this!' she protested. 'I need a shower and—'

'Five minutes,' he interrupted very firmly, all trace of amusement gone from his voice. 'I'll wait for you out in my car.'

As Kaycee hesitated there was another loud banging

of pots and pans from the kitchen. He raised an eye-brow at her.

Reluctantly she shook her head. 'Rowan, I just can't go and leave Mum. One of the reasons I left work was to try and talk to her. She. . .she's just dropped this bombshell about the house completely out of the blue and. . .and Drew has to be told before he goes back to Newcastle.'

Rowan frowned suddenly. 'But Drew knows about the house.'

'Drew knows?'

He frowned. 'It was Drew who told me after we'd finished in the tent and I was admiring the house. From what he said I understood he'd known for some time.'

He didn't add that he had felt worried for this woman when, with a concerned frown, her brother had told him, 'Mum's been wanting to sell for a long time. Then she made up her mind a few days ago, went to the real estate agent and has been in a real flap waiting for the right time to tell Kaycee. Then she told me this morning she blurted it right out in the middle of the party last night.'

Kaycee's dark brown eyes had widened with anger and then deep hurt. Rowan felt his heart contract as she stared at him and then one of her slender hands made a helpless gesture before she turned away.

He barely heard her choked-out words. 'All the years of trying to make ends meet; of being the strong, sensible one of the family—the *adult* of the family—apparently means nothing to Mum and Drew.'

Suddenly Rowan felt her pain as his own. He knew what it had cost this woman to put her own dreams and plans aside years ago so that her mother, sister and nine-year-old brother could live as she believed her father would have wanted. Now she was feeling as though all those years were being treated as insignificant—as though it gave her no right to be involved in the decision-making to sell their home.

He saw her tense and then she swung back to him. 'So you already knew about the house when you accepted Mum's invitation?' Her voice was low and filled with pain.

He hesitated briefly again and then said abruptly, 'Yes. As your mother pointed out, even if it was sold tomorrow it would take at least four to six weeks for the conveyancing to go through and contracts exchanged. It would give me more time to. . .' He paused briefly, and added quickly, 'To find suitable accommodation.'

To himself he added, And more time to get to know this fascinating woman.

He refused to entertain for more than a moment the thought that perhaps in some way he might be able to ease the burden she had carried for so long. A sudden memory of his own sister made him flinch. There had been nobody to ease her burden.

Kaycee was staring back at him with such a helpless look on her face that his hand lifted involuntarily and tucked a strand of hair behind one of her pale pink ears. His fingers lingered on her neck and he felt a tremor sweep through her.

'Don't look at me like that, Kaycee.' His voice was abrupt but he moved closer.

She looked down but not quickly enough to hide the expression that had flashed at him.

He groaned. 'Don't. I didn't want to cause you any more hurt.'

His hands seemed to have a mind of their own. They slid down her arms and then tugged gently. She raised tear-filled eyes. For a brief moment he felt her stiffen and then the tension seemed to flow out of her and she allowed him to press her closer.

Her head snuggled into his shoulder and he felt her body relax against him, accepting his comfort. It seemed perfectly natural for him to tilt her chin and gently claim her beautiful mouth. He felt her sudden stillness, her surprise. Then her lips softened and he was lost.

A truck horn blared from the driveway.

Rowan's eyes flew open. Kaycee's body stiffened against him. She wrenched herself out of his arms and he felt again the chill breeze swirl around him. Eyes as dazed as he felt stared back at him.

He opened his mouth but the sound of brakes squealing slightly made him swing around. A large truck was pulling to a stop not far from them. It had arrived to pick up the tent.

'Oh, no!' Kaycee's voice was choked. He swung back and watched her swallow rapidly. 'Where's Drew? He was supposed to be here to help.'

He clenched his teeth. Rowan Scott, you idiot! What on earth did you lose control like that for?

'He caught the early bus back to Newcastle after we brought your car back.'

As soon as the words were spoken he knew that they were too abrupt, too clipped.

'He's gone already?' Kaycee was looking anywhere but at his face. She tugged her gown closer. 'Look, would you ask them to wait while I change?'

'I told Drew I'd help.' Rowan felt her staring at him as he moved past her and towards the truck. He glanced back at her over his shoulder. 'Get your shower. I'll look after this.'

Without waiting for her response, he strode towards the truck as two men climbed out. He didn't like the smirk on the men's faces one little bit as he greeted them curtly. The tall, beer-bellied man grinned knowingly over Rowan's shoulder. Rowan swung back and scowled at the dressing-gowned figure in fluffy pink slippers. Kaycee blushed scarlet and then fled.

Rowan turned slowly back to the two men. He drew himself up and then didn't move; didn't say a word as he glared at them.

When at last the men started to look a little alarmed, he said with quiet emphasis, 'I'm Dr Scott. Miss Wiseman has not been well.'

'Treat 'em all with a kiss, do you, Doc?' the tall man said with a sneer. 'If that one's anything like her ma you should do OK there.'

Fury surged through Rowan. 'And you had better watch your mouth! Miss Wiseman is also a friend. And what you saw is absolutely none of your business. Do I make myself absolutely clear?'

Rowan felt his fists bunch and was tempted to take a swing at a jaw for the first time since school days and the Year Ten bully.

There was silence. The big man glared back at him.

'I'm also the only doctor in the town this weekend!' he warned in a controlled voice. With satisfaction he saw apprehension begin to replace the smirk and dropped his voice even more menacingly. 'So you'd better not have an accident on your way home.'

The younger man moved abruptly. 'Leave it, Tom,' he said curtly. 'My sister went to school with Kaycee Wiseman. She's certain that gossip was all a load of garbage about the Wisemans. Doc's right; it's none of our business.' He turned away. 'Let's get this stuff loaded up. We'll never get home at this rate.'

Rowan stared after them as they ambled away. 'I don't believe I said that!' he muttered out loud. He shook his head and turned and stared back at the house. 'And I don't believe that kiss!' Suddenly he grinned. 'Well, I wanted a change to the more personal country life and I sure have that!'

The men glared at him as he joined them and started helping to untie some ropes.

He shrugged a little apologetically. 'Must be the country air!'

The younger man straightened. His eyes began to twinkle, but his voice was quite serious as he drawled, 'Sure can do strange things to city blokes, I reckon.'

CHAPTER FOUR

KAYCEE let the warm water cascade over her. She grabbed the shampoo and rubbed it vigorously through her hair. But she couldn't get the expression on Rowan Scott's face out of her mind. When he had followed the truck drivers' gaze he had scowled at her ferociously and for the life of her she couldn't think why. It had not been her fault that he had pulled her into his arms and then kissed her so. . .so. . .

Automatically she rinsed, rubbed in some fragrant conditioner and rinsed again before grabbing a large towel. It wasn't until she lifted her head and looked in the mirror that she stopped her almost frantic movements.

She stared at the unusual bright colour and fullness of her lips. 'But you didn't have to let him make you lose it the way you did!' she muttered, and closed her eyes.

How was she going to face him again? She had allowed herself to be mesmerised by the gentle understanding that had filled his face. She had been helpless against the comfort and strength of those warm, strong hands that had closed around her and drawn her against him. She had let him cuddle her. . .so irresistibly. . .oh, so tenderly! Her body had suddenly developed a will of its own. Her lips had clung to his. They had devoured. They had opened. . .

Her hands still trembled. Her mind tumbled in confusion and embarrassment. That had been no ordinary kiss; certainly like nothing she had ever experienced before. What do you say to a man, especially one you've just met, after he has just kissed you senseless? Especially when you have just kissed him back. . .kissed him mindlessly!

What was I thinking? she thought frantically.

She straightened and turned away from the far too revealing mirror. Deliberately she tried to push away the memory of that kiss and marched down the corridor to her bedroom. It had happened. But that would be all. He had been feeling sorry for her. After all, he was the new doctor in town. She would have to work with him. And as for him living in the same house? Not if she could get out of it!

By the time she was almost dressed she had calmed down. But she still felt confused. She had to admit, no matter how reluctantly, that she would like the chance to get to know this attractive man on the more intimate level that sharing her home with him would mean.

Then she thought about the reaction she would get from the other staff at work when they found out where he was living. Then, of course, there was always that wretched gossip.

Despite her use of the hair dryer, Kaycee's hair was not completely dry when she impatiently decided that she had been inside too long. Normally she kept the shining swath of hair tightly controlled in a chignon at work or in a long pony-tail. Now in a hurry to make sure her help was not needed, she left it flowing free again as she hurried outside.

The breeze had freshened again and, although she had dressed in a pair of trousers and a warm cardigan, she gave a shiver, wishing that she had used the hair dryer a little longer.

When she came up to the truck Rowan turned from talking to the driver. He glanced at her and then stared, motionless.

She tugged at the edges of her cardigan, pulling it across her. Something flared in his eyes and she self-consciously tucked a wayward strand of damp hair behind her ear. His eyes blazed even brighter. Thoroughly embarrassed, she hunched her shoulders.

'Well, I'll be off, then.'

They both started and turned sharply towards the man with the huge sign, PARTY FOR HIRE, sprawled across his jacket.

'Miss Wiseman? We'll be sending our account to you through the mail. It's a seven-day account.'

There was a stern, warning note in the man's voice and Kaycee forced herself to pay attention.

'No.' She cleared her voice and said emphatically. 'No, not here. Send the account to Bob Gould in Taree. I believe he ordered it from you.'

The man hesitated for a moment and then dragged out an order book from his bulky jacket. 'No, a Mrs Wiseman from this address placed the order.' He looked up and glared at Kaycee. 'Any problem with that?'

Kaycee lifted her chin but before she could speak the deep voice beside her said calmly, 'No problem at all, Tom. I'm sure if you send it here it will be sorted out.'

As the truck began bumping its way slowly down the driveway, Kaycee let out a hissed breath. 'And who gave you the right to butt in?'

Rowan stared back silently at her. Then he shook his head slightly and shrugged. 'No one, I guess. Except your mother said—'

'My mother's said far too much already!'

Rowan straightened. Ice flowed from his expression as he surveyed her furious face. 'You were right. You've obviously got a lot of problems to sort out. And not only with your mother, I would say. I'd better go.'

As he turned towards his car Kaycee found her voice. 'But. . .but what about. . .? Are you going to board here?' she called after him.

'I doubt it very much,' the tall figure tossed over his shoulder at her without pausing in his long stride.

Dismay and a deep, unreasonable feeling of loss replaced her anger as she watched him disappear into the beautiful red car. Then, without even a wave to her, he was gone.

'He's right, Kaycee. You do have a lot of problems to sort out.'

Kaycee stiffened and then spun around. Her mother was standing several feet away in the shade of a large, flowering red bottle-brush tree.

Later Kaycee blamed her horrible words on the flood of anger and frustration that swept over her, coupled with a sudden feeling of weariness and depression.

'*I* have a lot of problems to sort out? If that's the case, you're my biggest problem!' she blurted out furiously.

As soon as the words left her mouth Kaycee was horrified that she could be so cruel. Thank goodness Rowan had left!

Mrs Wiseman's face flushed with outrage and then a look of anguish filled her eyes.

Kaycee opened her mouth to apologise but her mother whispered, 'I know but I've been trying to put that right.'

Regret and shame hit Kaycee at her mother's obvious

distress. She took a step forward and put out a beseeching hand. 'Oh, Mum! I'm so sorry, I——'

'Don't say another word, Kaycee.' With an obvious effort Mrs Wiseman straightened her shoulders. Her voice was so filled with unusual authority that Kaycee was silenced. 'And there's really nothing to discuss about this house. I've been thinking for some time that it would be best for all of us, especially you, if it was sold. Any time I've ever mentioned it over the years you've dismissed it out of hand.

'I know how much you fought in the beginning to keep up the payments on the mortgage. I also know how much it is costing still in rates and maintenance. But it still belongs to me and I can do what I want with it. You'll be compensated.'

'Can't I even ask what your reasons are for selling?' Kaycee asked in a choked voice.

'Yes, you can,' her mother said shortly, 'but I'm in no mood now to explain. I started to tell you last night that Bob has asked me to marry him. That is by no means my main reason for selling this house but you flew right off the handle at me last night when I started to tell you. I'm sorry. I know last night was the wrong time to tell you but there never seemed to be a right time.

'Now is not the right time to talk about it either. I'm too. . .too upset with you.' With that she turned and marched back into the house, letting the screen door slam behind her.

Utterly bewildered, Kaycee stared after her. Not since her father's heart attack in his late forties had her mother taken the reins into her own hands. In fact, Kaycee could not ever remember a time when she had been quite like this before. And so it was true. She was going to marry Bob Gould, that quiet, insignificant-looking middle-aged man that Kaycee had never been able to take seriously. Not after her wonderful father.

Suddenly feeling a desperate need to be alone, she turned and followed the path that led to the back vegetable garden and small orchard. She paused beneath a gnarled old peach tree. Its blooms were almost finished and, regretfully, she noted how badly it needed pruning.

Her father had planted these fruit trees and established the vegetable garden. Her mother had never been interested in anything except the flower garden. She had been responsible for the colourful shrubs and annuals planted each year at the front entrance. But Kaycee had enlisted her brother's and sister's help to keep the vegetable garden going after their father had died.

Some years they had even been able to supplement her income by the sale of fresh vegetables to friends and neighbours.

She sighed as she looked around. Since Jan had married last year and with Drew gone all this year the large expanse of lawns and the garden had been neglected. Drew had used the sit-on mower a couple of times on his rare weekends home earlier in the year.

On her own days off there had been so many other things to do inside the house that there had been little time to spend outdoors. Fortunately Bob Gould had tidied the front so that it had looked nice for the party.

Thoughtfully Kaycee kicked at a clump of milk thistles.

Over the years since her father's death her mother had never contributed much to the running of the house and grounds. And, then, these last couple of months especially, her mother had rarely been at home, spending a lot of time with her friend at his place in Taree.

She sighed. After Drew's party Kaycee had been hoping to at least be able to plant a few carrots and even peas. Now it would only be a waste of time if the house was to be sold.

It was a beautiful afternoon and impulsively she bent and tugged at another thistle in last season's lettuce bed. That led to another and before she knew it she was on her knees, mindlessly clearing a large patch of rich, dark soil. The mechanical action of pulling out weeds was soothing and the time passed quickly.

When at last she climbed to her feet she surveyed the cleared area with satisfaction. She brushed the dirt from her hands and pulled a face. Gloves and a digging fork would have been far more practical.

Hesitantly she glanced back at the house. Still not ready for another session with her mother, she made for the gate in the back fence. It gave access to the track through the bush that led down to the small creek that ambled its way through the gully a couple of kilometres from the house.

It had been a fairly dry and sunny winter and, although the last few days had turned colder, the spring wild flowers were in full bloom. The scrub thickened around her and she paused to listen to the birdsong, acknowledging a little sadly that it had always been one of her favourite places.

'Wonder if a city bloke like Rowan Scott would like this walk,' she muttered out loud.

A little shocked to realise how close he still was to her thoughts, she glanced around self-consciously. A parrot's screech startled her and there was a flash of red and green as a couple of them raced to find more delectables to eat among the blossoms.

Several minutes later she had almost reached the
creek when she heard the squeal and then laughter of
children. She paused, listening for a moment for adult
voices and not wanting to intrude. After a moment
she frowned and quickened her pace, pushing her way
through the bush that had encroached on the now sel-
dom used track beside the creek.

They sounded like very young children. There would
be very little water in the creek after the recent dry
spell but it was still not a very safe place for small
children to play without adult supervision.

Just as she saw the two small figures crouched down
a couple of metres from the bank of the creek one of
them cried out and jumped back, shaking a finger. 'It
bitted me!'

'Ah, don't be a baby; they're only little.' The slightly
bigger boy's voice was scornful as he peered into a
large white plastic bucket on the ground.

They both glanced up and looked warily at Kaycee
as she approached.

'Hello,' she said cheerfully. 'What have you found?'

They stood up, the older boy moving to stand protec-
tively in front of the smaller one. As he gripped a small,
sturdy stick he glared at her silently.

But the small boy pushed his way to the front. His
face was full of excitement. 'We's found some worms.
Real big ones. You wanna look?'

But Kaycee needed no invitation to look. She had
already frozen in horror as she peered into the old
bucket. Several 'worms' were squirming over each
other, trying frantically to escape up the steep sides.

Only they weren't big worms; they weren't even
worms. They were baby snakes, baby Eastern brown
snakes by the look of them, and highly venomous.

Kaycee looked quickly around and spotted an old rotten log. The ground and leaves near it had obviously been scratched at. Fearfully she scanned the thick grass nearby.

She took a deep breath and pointed. 'Did you find them over there?'

Her voice was sharp and the boys took a step back. Silently she berated herself as the older boy said belligerently, 'We're not allowed to talk to strangers.'

Obviously ready to bolt, he grabbed the hand of the other boy and bent down to pick up their treasure.

'Don't touch them!' Kaycee cried out urgently.

She rushed forward and gave a hefty kick. Container and baby snakes went flying off into the bush in all directions.

Both boys gave a bellow of rage and protest but before either could dash to pick them up Kaycee had grabbed them by their T-shirts.

Trying to control her mounting panic, she forced a grin. 'Sorry, boys, but I'm afraid they aren't worms.' She took a deep breath. 'They're baby snakes and one or both of their parents probably aren't too far away. But even baby snakes can be very dangerous. I heard you say one had bitten you.'

As they still tried to pull away from her she added in as controlled a voice as she could, 'Please, you must let me see. Look, if you've been bitten you could get very sick,' she added a little desperately as they stopped struggling and stared blankly at her. 'I'm a nurse at the hospital and I know.'

'I got bit on my finger.' The smallest boy held up a finger for inspection.

Kaycee's heart plunged as she saw two definite puncture marks. Her mind raced. She had read exten-

sively about snake bites after a patient had almost died
from one a few years ago. The first rule of first aid was
to try and keep the victim as calm as possible.

But nobody had told her how the one doing the first
aid could stay calm!

Hoping that they could not sense her growing panic,
she reached out and gently held the small arm. 'Any
more bites?'

He shook his head, his eyes wide. The other boy
scowled at her silently. Kaycee could see the suspicion
in his face.

Scared that he might still race off, she forced a smile.
'What are your names?'

'I'm Brett and he's Stevie,' the older boy growled.
'He's me little brother and I look after 'im good,' he
added belligerently. 'I've got an headache and we was
just goin' home.'

Thinking furiously, Kaycee said as gently as she
could, 'He's a very fortunate little boy to have a brother
like you.'

She thought that she remembered reading once that
the amount of venom in a baby snake was as much as
in an adult to give it as much protection as nature could
in its most vulnerable stage. A pressure bandage to stop
the venom reaching the lymphatic system should be
applied as soon as possible.

'I don't suppose you'd have a handkerchief?' she
asked hopefully as she dragged her own clean one out
and rapidly wrapped it tightly around the small finger
and hand as best she could to immobilise it.

They both shook their heads. 'What ya' doin' that
for?' Brett asked, a hint of fear now in his voice.

'Trying to stop the poison from the snake bite
making your brother sick. Boys, where do you live?'

Her heart sank as Brett told her the address of the new housing estate, a good twenty minutes' walk and uphill all the way. Although it had only taken her several minutes to walk down the steep incline to the creek the climb back up would take longer, especially carrying the boy. But hopefully it would be faster than to the housing estate.

'Does your mother know where you are?' Her voice was a little sharper and she swallowed as they stared back at her.

'No,' said Stevie in a scared little voice. 'We was havin' an 'venture.'

'Well, you're certainly having that,' Kaycee said grimly. She crouched down and looked Brett in the eye. 'Do you understand that we've got to get help for your brother as quickly as we can or he could get very, very sick from the poison from the snake?'

His face was now very pale as he gave a brief nod.

'Right, I've got to carry him and we've got to go as fast as we can back to my house.' As she saw the protest and increasing panic in his face, she added firmly, 'It's closer than your home and I'll ring your mum.'

She picked up the small boy, a little relieved to find he was lighter than he looked.

'Brett got bit too,' a scared little voice whispered in her ear.

Kaycee stared at him and then put him down hurriedly.

'Brett! Where did you get bitten?' she asked a little hysterically, 'and how long ago?'

There was no answer to her last question as Brett hesitated and then pointed to his feet. 'They didn't hurt much,' he said in a whisper.

To Kaycee's absolute horror there was more than

one set of fang marks on the top of his bare left foot.
You fool, she castigated herself silently, you should
have guessed! As she bent to examine them she could
see that they were like needle jabs and very fine. There
could be more.

And then Kaycee gasped in horror as Brett swayed,
muttered, 'I feel sick,' and promptly was.

That answered the question she was so worried
about. He had been bitten long enough before for the
venom to have started affecting him.

Afterwards Kaycee had nightmares about her frantic
dash through the bush with the smaller boy clinging
piggyback style to her while she held Brett in her arms.
By the time that the house came in sight Brett had been
sick again and he was a dead weight. Her muscles were
aching badly and she had hardly any breath left to call
out as she collapsed at the back steps, dropping the
boys on the grass.

Then her mother was beside her, exclaiming in
dismay.

'Snake bite,' Kaycee gasped, struggling up. 'Will
you grab some bandages while I bring the car?'

'Both of them?' her mother groaned in horror.

Kaycee nodded breathlessly. By the time she had
brought the small yellow car as close as she could to
the back door her mother was rapidly rolling an elastic
bandage tightly around Brett's foot and up his leg.
Thank goodness her mother had done that first-aid
course with her.

Without undoing the handkerchief, Kaycee was
rapidly doing the same to Stevie's arm when Mrs
Wiseman said in a low, carefully controlled voice, 'The
bites on the foot were starting to bleed slightly.'

Kaycee froze momentarily and stared across at her

mother. Already! That meant that it had been some time since. . .

As Kaycee swung Stevie onto the front seat he began crying loudly.

'Shush, darling, Brett's coming too.'

Mrs Wiseman deposited her burden on the back seat and hesitated. 'Brett's pretty dazed, Kaycee. I should come with you.'

For a moment Kaycee hesitated too and then shook her head. 'No, I think it's more important to have a doctor and antivenin waiting at the hospital. Tell them they looked like Eastern brown snakes.'

Her mother still paused a moment but then hurried off as Kaycee started the car. She was aching and still breathing rapidly. Her whole body was trembling as the car jolted down the track to the main road as fast as she dared to drive.

'Don't cry, Stevie,' she said soothingly to the little boy even as she glanced over her shoulder at Brett, wishing he was well enough to cry. 'We'll have you to a nice doctor very soon.'

Please, she prayed silently, let that be true. I hope you aren't far from your beeper, Rowan Scott!

CHAPTER FIVE

Rowan had just walked back to his car in the practically deserted main street when his pager went off.

As Mrs Wiseman had warned him, the search for a real estate agent that might be open on a Sunday afternoon was fruitless. With a weary sigh he unhooked the contraption from his belt but waited until he was half sitting in the car before reading the flashing message.

Thank goodness it had a digital read-out and not just one that meant he had to find a phone or go straight to the hospital. All he needed was to have an emergency at the hospital with no other doctor in town until late tonight! And that was another thing he had not thought of. He needed a mobile phone.

Two Snake Bites to Hospital from Wisemans.

He stared at the flashing message. For the first time in many, many years he came very close to panicking.

The sports car started with a roar and took off with a Sydney city-driver's speed—right in front of a startled farmer in his battered utility. Completely unaware of the muttered imprecations that followed him, Rowan's hands clenched on the steering wheel as he took the first bend much too fast.

'Snake bite! Why does it have to be snake bite?'

The words burst from him even as he negotiated the next bend with a squeal of tyres.

'God! Let them have more than one ampoule of antivenin in this small hospital!'

In a matter of moments he saw the little yellow car

barrelling along. As he saw Kaycee's hand go out to wave him down a tremendous feeling of relief swept through him. At least she could still drive.

He stopped his car well off the road in a screech of brakes and a cloud of dust. By the time Kaycee's car had pulled up he had the driver's door open. His hand clutched at her arm.

And then he saw them.

Kids!

His heart lurched violently as he took in the state of the biggest boy lying down on the back seat. Fiercely he fought for control.

'The boy in the back, he. . .he. . .'

Kaycee's frantic voice pierced through his black memories. The training of years took over. He raced around to scoop out the small, round-eyed boy from the front seat and scrambled into the back with him. The bigger boy stared at him from dazed, pain-filled eyes.

'Get going,' he said crisply, 'I've got them.'

As the car picked up speed again there came the sound of vomiting. Kaycee glanced quickly over her shoulder. It was Stevie this time but then Brett started again as well. To her relief Rowan was dealing with it very capably, using the towels that her mother had thrown in at the last moment. His voice was gentle and soothing. For a moment she had seen blind panic darken his face when he had seen the kids.

Then she realised that he was speaking to her in a well-controlled voice, 'Names, please.'

For a moment fright and strain closed up her throat.

'Kaycee, don't you dare go all female on me,' the deep face said with a snap, even as she took a bend a little too quickly. 'And drive carefully! You won't achieve anything by having an accident.'

Indignation swept through her. Female!

Through gritted teeth she snapped, 'Stevie and Brett. I don't know their last name.' She swallowed rapidly. 'Stevie was just sick. I only saw one bite on him.' She gulped and her voice shook. 'Brett has multiple bites. They started to bleed a few minutes ago. . .as Mum bandaged him. . .'

A grunt was her only answer as there was the sound of more vomiting.

After a moment he asked, 'Why didn't your mother come with you?'

Kaycee bit her lip. 'I. . .I thought it better if she phoned. . .'

'Not if the respiratory muscles started to seize up.'

A shudder passed through Kaycee as she acknowledged the truth of what he had said. And her mother could have coped, Kaycee acknowledged suddenly. She had changed so much recently.

Something hard lodged in Kaycee's throat.

After she had regained control of her voice, she murmured, 'How. . .how did you get here so quickly?'

'Hospital paged me a few minutes ago. I was in town,' he said abruptly. 'Now, concentrate on driving!'

It was the shortest trip that Kaycee had ever made to the hospital. But even so, Brett was very drowsy by the time they rushed him into the emergency department.

As the boys were carried to adjoining cubicles Rowan grabbed her by the arm as they followed.

'What type of snake?' he snapped.

'Baby ones,' Kaycee managed to gasp.

He glared at her impatiently and she took a quick breath, clasping her shaking hands to try and steady them. She knew that he was asking for a positive identification for the correct antivenin.

'Because they were so small, I'm not certain. They certainly weren't black red bellies. Either Eastern brown or tiger. They were very pale brown with stripes.'

Rowan turned to his small patient and reached for the tourniquet off the waiting IV tray. 'Hold his arm for me, Kaycee. What antivenin have you?' he snapped at the waiting Sister Allen. He let out a sigh of relief as she answered crisply, 'Polyvalent and monovalent for all known species in the area.'

'How many ampoules?'

'Three polyvalent and one each of the monovalents,' he was told. 'Two polyvalent are on that tray. The venom detection kit is ready also if you want to use it first,' Sister Allen added crisply.

Kaycee saw his tense shoulders relax slightly. He had picked up an intravenous cannula and was bent over the small arm before he said, 'Unusual to have so much in a hospital this size, isn't it?'

Sister Allen shrugged slightly and Kaycee said quietly, 'We nearly lost a snake-bite victim a few years ago. There was only one polyvalent and no detection kit then.'

Rowan glanced up at her briefly. 'We'll need at least two ampoules for each boy, possibly even more for Brett.'

He finished inserting the cannula as a nurse completed placing monitor lines onto the small figure. 'Normal saline to dilute the antivenin, Sister?'

Sister Allen had it ready also but she asked quietly, 'The test first?'

Rowan hesitated for a moment. He glanced over at Stevie who was now crying noisily.

'I don't want to waste any time, especially with this older boy. We'll give each a dose of polyvalent first and when that's through test to see which monovalent antivenin is the right one for the rest. I know that monovalents don't have as many side-effects. Sister, would you get onto the emergency departments in Newcastle, please? We'll need more ampoules.'

As he was speaking, he had started to efficiently insert another IV cannula into Brett's other arm. He tossed crisply over his shoulder at Kaycee, 'Any idea how long since they were bitten and what first aid?'

'I heard Stevie say he'd been bitten just as I found them about. . .' she glanced at her watch, amazed at how little time had really gone '. . .about forty minutes or so ago. I don't know about Brett. I think it must have been some time. He already had a headache,' Kaycee said helplessly, 'and then he started vomiting. . .'

She shuddered at the horror of reliving that moment and watched Rowan insert the second IV cannula as she held Brett's arm. She thought for a moment and then remembered that had been one other thing that that poor young doctor had been roared at by old Dr Gordon for not doing for that other snake-bite victim.

Despite the risk of bleeding from IV sites an immediate intravenous access was needed for taking blood for tests. Another line was also required for treating any severe allergic reaction to the antivenin as it entered the bloodstream.

Then Rowan was diluting the antivenin with the required amount of normal saline.

'I. . .I only had a handkerchief.' As she continued

Kaycee's voice quivered so much that she bit her lip hard for a moment, trying to control herself before adding, 'They. . .they were starting to get really scared and I didn't want to panic them any more or waste time by starting to tear up clothes. But it took me ages to get them home. Mum put on Brett's bandage while I got the car. You won't undo them yet, will you?' she asked agitatedly, and then gulped at the glare Rowan flung her way.

Obviously he was very aware of one of the first principles of emergency hospital snake-bite treatment she had learnt a few years ago when that forest walker had been admitted. If a bite was certain and there was definite envenomation, as the boys were showing, the pressure bandage was not to be removed until after antivenin was administered.

'Did you wash the sites or cut them and try to suck out the poison?' he rapped out.

'Of course not,' she snapped back indignantly. Anybody who had done the first-aid course that she had would know such basic stuff.

It had been found that venom on the skin would not be absorbed and washing only made obtaining venom for testing from the bite practically impossible. Studies had shown years ago that cutting the fang marks only removed a small amount of venom anyway and there was real danger of the first-aid giver also being poisoned through the mouth.

Rowan looked up at her for a brief moment and she saw the relief in his eyes.

Only then did Kaycee realise that he had been worried about the possibility of her being poisoned also if she had done the first aid used so widely years ago.

Thank goodness that experiments had proved that

all that was needed was to apply a constrictive bandage
that would not stop arterial or venous pressure. It had
to be around the bite sight, down and then up the limb,
preferably with a splint to immobilise it. This delayed
the central movement of the venom into the lymph
system.

'Did I do the right things?' she suddenly blurted out
anxiously. Rowan already thought that she had made
the wrong choice with her mother. 'Should I have
stopped to try and rip up one of the boys' T-shirts before
racing back to the house? My own thick fleecy-lined
cardigan was far too bulky. Should I have wasted precious moments trying to find something to splint
their limbs?'

She fought back the tears as sudden exhaustion swept
over her. A firm, masculine hand grabbed her as she
swayed and then she was sitting on a chair trying to
catch her breath out of the way of the activity around
the two cubicles.

She heard Rowan say crisply above her head to
someone, 'Neuro obs, please. Adrenaline handy? Why
isn't that oxygen on yet? Is that a paediatric
endotracheal tube?'

She looked up at him through a sudden mist of tears
but although it had been his hands that had grabbed
her his attention was still on Brett.

Then he glanced down at her. 'I'm quite sure you
did all you could as fast as you could,' he murmured
gently.

For a brief moment their eyes clung.

Then Kaycee looked away. 'I'm OK,' she muttered.

He nodded briefly and moved over to Stevie. While
he had been with Brett, Sister Allen had returned from
phoning and started trying to cannulate Stevie. That

young man's crying had now become a full-blown roar of pain and fright, only interrupted by another bout of vomiting. The nurse who had been assisting had been forced to race off to answer the phone.

'Stevie, I thought you were going to be a big brave boy like Brett,' Rowan said firmly and perhaps a little unfairly as Brett was far too sick to make any fuss. 'Come on, little man,' Kaycee heard him add very gently, 'we have to give you some medicine to make you better.'

But Stevie's roars only increased.

Kaycee stood up a little shakily. 'Could I hold him for you?'

Rowan frowned and then nodded reluctantly. 'I've got to get the polyvalent into Brett but we've got to get this little fellow's IV lines in too. Being upset like this is spreading that venom too fast. I don't want to sedate him just yet unless we have to. It's easier to check conscious levels and any paralysis.'

As he was speaking, Kaycee picked up the small boy. Terrified, Stevie clung to her but gradually she was able to soothe him enough so that it wasn't long before the two lots of antivenin were dripping very slowly through both IV lines.

'I read once that antihistamine and adrenaline are given before commencing polyvalent in case of a severe reaction to the serum,' Kaycee murmured uncertainly, in an agony of suspense as they watched and listened to the beep of the monitors and the slow drip of the IV.

Rowan's glance pierced her.

Heat flushed her cheeks and she inwardly groaned. She was doing it again, questioning his expertise.

'Nurse Wiseman, I do believe Dr Scott knows what he's doing.' Sister Allen's voice was sharp.

To Kaycee's relief, Rowan suddenly smiled. 'Yes, I do, thank you, Sister. But it's natural for Kaycee to feel protective of her little charges. Besides, she's right.' Then he frowned thoughtfully. 'Actually, there are two major viewpoints about that. One group, including the antivenin manufacturer, recommends the routine use of premedication, especially subcutaneous adrenaline and an antihistamine to reduce the chance of anaphylaxis.' He paused and then he admitted, 'It's considered particularly useful for country doctors.'

His eyes were darting from one small face to the other, carefully monitoring them for any adverse reactions. 'So far so good,' he muttered, and leaned over and speeded up Brett's drip a little. 'It has to run through in fifteen to twenty minutes, Sister,' he added.

Then he continued. 'The opposing view is that such premedication is potentially hazardous as it may cause hypertension and drowsiness or irritability which can obscure signs of envenomation and may not be effective in practice in preventing anaphylaxis.'

He sounds like a textbook, Kaycee thought a little crossly, but then a gleam of amusement briefly lit up his eyes. To her astonishment he winked at her behind Sister's back as that capable woman leaned over to adjust an oxygen mask.

This encouraged Kaycee to voice her other concern but she frowned, wondering what Sister Allen would say.

'You've got another problem, Nurse Wiseman?' Rowan said very gently.

She looked at him uncertainly, wishing that she could see his eyes to see if that stern look was back in them that had been there that morning, despite the gentle tones.

'They're only small children,' she blurted out. 'You're giving them each the whole ampoule and talking about more. Isn't. . .isn't that the adult dose?'

She saw Rowan stiffen and braced herself for his anger but he merely said grimly, 'Children require the same dose as adults.' He drew a quick breath and looked across at her. For a moment a vulnerable, haunted look crossed his face.

'Believe me, I know! When I was a kid one of my friends died from snake bite. Apparently he wasn't given enough antivenin. They know now that the effects of the poison can recommence. After the state of shock ceases the venom can be released more into the system.

'So far so good,' Rowan added quickly as Sister turned around. 'These two look like being part of the ninety per cent who don't have a severe reaction. We'll let Stevie's continue a little slower than his brother's. When the ampoules are through keep the line open with normal saline until we get the results of the venom detection test. We'll do that as fast as we can but I don't want to even cut a hole in the pressure bandage to take a sample until at least one ampoule is in each of the boys' systems—possibly even two for the larger boy.'

Kaycee relaxed, convinced that Rowan was no stranger to snake-bite treatment even though the sister-in-charge was. She had been at the hospital for a few years and was very capable and efficient but snake bites were relatively rare.

In the eight years that Kaycee had worked here there had only ever been that one snake-bite victim—a bush walker in the state forest. It had been a couple of hours before he had reached hospital. The venom had already been causing muscle paralysis. Muscles in the throat and chest had deteriorated first and he had been put immediately onto a resuscitation machine.

There had only been one ampoule each of the polyvalent and the monovalents in the hospital. Luckily they had been able to give him both but it had been touch and go until more serum arrived. Fortunately the young doctor had immediately organised the rescue helicopter to bring more even before the man had arrived at the hospital.

Even more fortunately the man had been bitten through a thick woollen sock so that he had not had as much poison as he might have. Then, much to the relief of the staff, the patient had been flown to the toxicology unit in Newcastle.

They had found out later that he had still needed a life-support system for some time. The poison had caused muscles to be destroyed and parts of the muscle tissue had caused blockages in his kidneys. He had needed dialysis for quite a while after. Fortunately there had been no thrombosis to cause further major problems and he had eventually recovered. He had been fortunate. Several people died of snake bites each year in Australia.

Kaycee shuddered. Stevie should be OK but she suspected that it would be a while before they could be sure about Brett.

Thank goodness it was not only obvious that Rowan was very familiar with emergency hospital treatment for snake bite but also with the effects on a child. Obviously at some time in his career he had studied very carefully the treatment for snake bite. And he was very good with the little boys.

She watched him moving his large, strong hand soothingly over Brett's little head. His gentle, comforting smile made Kaycee hold her breath for a moment in wonder. Then she looked swiftly away. Pull yourself together, girl. You don't even know if he has a wife and child of his own somewhere. Just because he needs board just for himself doesn't mean. . .

She gulped.

She had taken for granted that he was not married because he needed board for himself; because he had kissed her. But perhaps there was a wife and child somewhere. Perhaps. . .

No! All her instincts told her that he was not the kind of man to kiss another woman as he had her if he was married.

Suddenly he looked up at her. His face was very serious as his gaze swept over her and then held her eyes. She felt a tide of warmth rush into her face but refused to look away.

Then his eyes softened. A gentle, intimate smile spread across his face. She felt her own lips move in response before she looked hastily away, suddenly confused at the silent communication that had leapt like sparks of electricity across the space between them.

Suddenly she had a burning desire to know everything about him. Every little detail about him as a man, as a doctor—his likes, his dislikes.

All the gossip had given little indication of his personal background—only that he had held a position in a renowned hospital as a surgical registrar.

She remembered the speculation that had been sweeping the hospital over the past week. Why would a budding surgeon want to do a country locum as a GP?

Rowan's quiet voice interrupted her thoughts. 'Any success contacting the children's parents, Sister?'

'When we rang the police they said they'd get a car out to that area and make enquiries as soon as they could but. . .'

There was a slight commotion at the entrance to the emergency department and they simultaneously glanced around.

'Mum, what are you—?' Kaycee broke off as a distraught woman brushed past her mother where she hesitated in the doorway.

'My boys!' the woman exclaimed in a voice filled with fear. 'Cathryn said that they'd been bitten— oh, no!'

Rowan moved quickly towards the woman as she rushed forward, her eyes pinned on the boys surrounded by tubes and lines.

'Stevie's and Brett's mother?' he asked crisply, and then added rapidly, 'We're just giving them both a dose of general-purpose snake antivenin before testing the venom to see if we can identify the type of snake for their next dose.'

Kaycee had placed Stevie back on the bed once the drips had commenced. But he had refused to let her go and had been clutching her hand tightly. But now, hearing his mother's voice, he tried to sit up and promptly started vomiting again.

The woman moaned with fear and started forward but Rowan clasped her arm. 'Let Nurse handle it and then you can sit between the beds and be near both boys. I think he's being sick from fright and shock as much as from poisoning.'

He continued calmly explaining what was being

done for her sons until Kaycee had finished holding the basin for Stevie and cleaned him up.

Rowan nodded briefly at Kaycee as she at last made way for the mother. He said softly, 'Don't go until I've had a chance to speak to you, Nurse Wiseman,' and then continued to explain why Brett was more badly affected than his smaller brother.

Kaycee hurried over to her mother. 'Mum, what are you doing here?'

'I drove Shirley Porter to the hospital.' Mrs Wiseman gestured to the boys' mother.

'You know her?'

'Yes, of course,' Mrs Wiseman said a little impatiently, her eyes fastened on the group near the boys. 'They moved here from Sydney a couple of months ago when her husband was transferred. I stopped by once when I saw her trying to start her new garden. Thought she might like some cuttings. I recognised the boys straight away.'

Kaycee wondered why she should have felt surprised. It was so typical of Coolong. No one could remain strangers very long.

'She'd already been going round the neighbours trying to find the little villains,' Mrs Wiseman continued. 'When I drove up someone had just told her they saw them walking towards the creek.' She paused and whispered anxiously, 'Do you know if they're going to be OK?'

Without hesitation Kaycee murmured, 'I'm sure they will be. Rowan knows what he's doing.'

Her mother glanced at her sharply. Feeling a little uncomfortable, Kaycee wondered why she'd answered with such certainty. There was just something about the man and the doctor that inspired confidence.

Mrs Wiseman returned her attention to the group around the cubicles. 'The poor little darlings. Shirley told me that all the kids in their area are older—school age. They get bored quickly. Now, do you think that Sister would let me use the phone? Shirley wants me to try and track down her husband. He's working out in the bush today. Hopefully his office can help.'

A slightly bemused Kaycee watched her mother stride over to the nurses' desk and tackle Sister Allen. Staff did not like the phone tied up with outside calls but Kaycee grinned slightly as she saw her mother speaking rapidly and then reach out and pick up the phone.

Then she sobered and stared at her mother thoughtfully. Her mother was certainly exhibiting more initiative and increasing assertiveness and confidence than Kaycee could remember for years. More evidence of the influence of Bob Gould? If so it was a good influence, Kaycee decided a little reluctantly.

It was some time before Rowan was free to speak to Kaycee again. His keen eyes swept over her face as she wearily pushed back her hair at his approach.

'I need to rescue my car from the side of the road. Is there anyone you can suggest I could contact to bring it to the hospital? It will be dark very soon and I don't know how long I'll be here this evening,' he told her quietly.

That gorgeous red sports car? She gulped. 'Er. . .yes, of course,' she assured him hurriedly as a slight frown entered his eyes at her hesitancy. 'I'll organise it for you. Mum can drive me back to your car. She's just popped over to the wards to see Mr Rodgers and then she'll be back.'

Rowan looked concerned. 'But you're exhausted, Kaycee. Surely there's someone else?'

'And me miss out on driving that gorgeous car?' Kaycee grinned at him and then sobered. 'Unless of course you don't trust me with it?'

He considered her silently. A gleam entered his eyes. 'Oh, yes, I trust you. . .with the car,' he murmured. Then he reached into his pocket and tossed a set of keys to her. Crisply he added, 'Go straight away. I'll make sure your mother doesn't leave without you. And I told your mother just before that I would take her up on her offer of board. You don't need to move any of your things because Drew did say I could use his room.'

A strange sense of relief flooded through Kaycee. The strength of that relief suddenly worried her and she scowled.

Before she could speak Rowan added wearily, 'I'm sorry you don't approve but it seems I have no choice. Even the motel is booked out because of the cattle sale tomorrow.'

Before she could reassure him someone called, 'Dr Scott, phone!'

He strode rapidly away, leaving Kaycee trembling with a multitude of mixed emotions. For a moment she watched him as he picked up the phone. She heard him confirming that more antivenin was on its way. The relief in his voice told her how worried he still was about the boys, especially Brett.

Kaycee hesitated, reluctant to leave until she knew for sure that they would be all right. It was so essential that a sufficient quantity of the right antivenin was given in time. Then common sense took over. There was nothing further that she could do here and he was right—she was feeling very weary.

Briefly she wondered at the instant relief and, yes, something like delight that the thought of him staying with them had brought her.

But, as she turned away and made her way out of the hospital, trepidation slowly filled her once again. Something told her that it would not be very wise living in such close proximity with this dynamic man. And what would the gossiping staff at the hospital think? Her world had already been turned upside down during the last twenty-four hours. She had a sinking feeling that the near future could get much worse.

But as she drove his car back to the hospital, surrounded by the already somehow familiar fragrance that was Rowan Scott, the main feeling that trickled through every part of her being was anticipation. She would have a chance to get to know more about this fascinating man in a personal way as well as professionally.

And perhaps. . .perhaps one day he just might want to kiss her again.

CHAPTER SIX

IT WAS well after midnight before Rowan drove slowly over the rough track to the Wisemans' house. He winced as the car once again scraped on a rut in the road. This second-hand sports car had been part of the fulfilment of a boyhood dream but not very practical for a country practice, he acknowledged with a deep, exhausted sigh.

An outside light lit up the front entrance very well. He parked next to the small yellow car. Wearily he grabbed his case and climbed the steps to the front door. It stood wide open and the hall light was also still on. It was very welcoming and very different from city locks, he thought with a measure of satisfaction. He hesitated in the hallway for a moment, trying to get his bearings and remember where Mrs Wiseman had said her son's room was. A soft light glowed from a door opposite the kitchen and he peered into the room.

An old Marx brothers movie was showing on a television and a slender figure, still in jeans and a fleecy-lined cardigan, was sound asleep on the lounge. Rowan put down his case and moved softly across and looked down at her. That glorious hair was spread out around her in abundant abandon. He caught his breath, remembering how—as the breeze had played with it— the bright sunlight had glowed on traces of fire.

He scowled. She was far too beautiful—and stubborn—for his peace of mind. And he was far too attracted to her after far too short a time. When he had given the Wisemans' phone number as a contact number he had not missed the quickly disguised surprise and speculation in the night sister's eyes. Only then had it hit him how his presence in Kaycee's home could be misinterpreted, especially in a small town like Coolong.

He had so quickly allowed himself to be drawn into her family and their problems. Somehow, this morning, that had strongly appealed to him. It all seemed a natural outcome of his desire to turn his back on the impersonal nature of large cities and return to country living.

He didn't have a very good track record of involvement with his own family. His own sister and her new husband were lucky to see him a couple of times a year now. It had been too many years since he had been part of a family; too many years since work had been allowed to become all-consuming, making him lose contact with family and old friends. And that had been one of Sonja's complaints too. He'd never had enough time for her.

And then tonight there had been that accident victim. Now he wasn't quite so sure that he was happy to become too involved with this family or this close-knit community when it could bring such pain.

He closed his eyes for a moment, remembering the shock and distress of the staff at the hospital a couple of hours earlier when the motorcyclist had been brought in. He had been well known in this small community, as no doubt most local accident victims would be.

He shuddered. Do I really want to become as involved as those poor nurses were tonight? That RN had gone to school with the teenager's mother.

And if I have to plunge into staying with a family,

why pick one who seems to have so many problems?

He chewed thoughtfully on his bottom lip as he examined the sleeping woman. There was something about Kaycee that intrigued him. In fact, each member of the Wiseman family intrigued him, he assured himself hastily. Andrew would have all the temptations of a first-year university student. The relationship between mother and daughter was obviously reaching some crisis point.

Kaycee moved slightly and then relaxed again.

In the soft light from a small lamp she looked far too young and vulnerable to have carried the family's burdens the way she must have for so many years. Her face was pale and anger, tinged with guilt, stirred within him.

She was just like Elle! How many times had he come home and found his sister waiting up for him? But, he told himself, this woman wasn't his sister and had no business waiting up for him when she must be so exhausted. He reached out and shook her gently by the shoulder. She sighed and settled herself more comfortably against the pillows.

'Here's where you should do your romantic bit and carry her to bed, and *her* bed, mate,' Rowan muttered impatiently to himself.

There were a few problems with that. He wasn't sure which room was hers. He was so darned tired he might drop her. And, besides all of that, she would probably smack his face if she woke up in his arms!

Then he suddenly worried about what would happen if instead she clasped those arms tightly around him and. . .

He crouched down beside her. 'Kaycee! Wake up, for goodness' sake!'

The exhaustion and anger in him made his voice much louder in the quiet room than he had intended and the grip on her arm too hard.

Long, dark eyelashes flew open and huge, sleep-filled eyes looked straight into his. His heart dipped.

Kaycee saw only the anger and impatience in Rowan's eyes and sat bolt upright. She looked away blindly and focused on the television. The old black and white movie had not finished so she could not have been asleep too long. She had tried so hard to stay awake but, despite her sleep in the middle of the day, the emotional and physical trauma had caught up with her.

'We. . .we expected you home hours ago.' Her voice was husky with sleep. Something flared in his eyes and she quickly looked away. 'Thank you for ringing earlier, though,' she added hurriedly.

Then the clouds of sleep disappeared further. She remembered that phone call and heat rushed into her face.

He had rung to warn them that he wouldn't be as late as he thought but not to expect him for a meal. Without letting him finish, she had said firmly, feeling much braver over the phone, 'I've moved my things into Drew's room so you can have the larger one.'

There had been dead silence at the other end of the phone.

'Look, its really all right. I'm feeling very bad about my attitude earlier,' she had added rapidly. 'I don't get anything done when he's home and his room really is too small for you to be charged the board Mum mentioned.'

'Thank you, Kaycee.' His voice had sounded husky. An urgent voice had demanded attention in the background and he had added crisply, 'I have to go. Shouldn't be too much longer.'

Ever since slowly hanging up the buzzing phone, she had been wondering if it would be wise living in close proximity to this disturbing man. Kaycee glanced at her watch. There must have been some other emergency for him to be so horribly late. And the poor man was still on call.

She glanced back up at him and the grim expression on his face made her suck in a deep breath. 'Rowan. . .'

He straightened slowly and just looked at her.

'What is it? Not Brett. . .?'

He shook his head abruptly. At the same time he brushed a large hand wearily over his face. 'I don't want to talk about it. I'm not sure I even should be here and I certainly didn't expect you to wait up for me.' His voice was unexpectedly harsh.

'Oh, I wasn't really.' Kaycee scrambled to her feet and moved over to switch off the television. 'There was an old movie on TV I wanted to watch.'

Which was almost the truth. She did like the Marx brothers but she had hardly smiled at their antics tonight, unable to concentrate as she had worried more and more about him the later it became. . . Worried more and more about that kiss near the tent. . . Worried more because of her unexpected and, she tried to convince herself, unwanted response to this man.

'I'll put the electric jug on and make you a cuppa. You must be—'

'Kaycee.'

His voice was so sharp that she spun round. He was very close and her body brushed against him. Nervously she took a step back. His hands came out and grasped her by the shoulders.

. 'Kaycee, if I'm going to board here I don't want you treating me like a guest. I don't want you waiting up for me. You've had an exhausting day yourself. You should be in bed. I didn't want you. . .' He paused.

Electricity darted through her.

His hands tightened and he gave her a slight shake. Anger darkened his eyes. 'I don't want you taking that kiss the wrong way. And I don't want you mothering me; staying up for me!'

'Take that kiss. . . Mothering you. . .!' For a moment she gaped at him. Then she twisted away from his touch. His hands dropped to his sides. 'I doubt if even your own mother would want to wait up for you,' she spat at him.

Something momentarily flashed into his eyes. Kaycee was too incensed then to take note of it.

Here she had been stewing for hours about seeing him again and he was angry she'd waited up for him!

Kaycee glared back at him. 'As for that kiss, may I remind you it wasn't me who started it.'

The black look on his face increased.

Stupid! she castigated herself. He knew darned well that she had participated fully in it.

She rushed on, 'And I only stayed up to make sure you knew where your room was. That you knew where things were in the kitchen. That you knew where the bathroom was. I stayed up for sheer common courtesy to a stranger in my home on his first night.' She swung away before he could see that she wasn't being absolutely honest and how much his words had hurt. 'Obviously not necessary. My apologies.'

She had taken three steps when he murmured, 'So you can say you're sorry.'

Almost she stopped.

Almost.

But she did not want him to see the tears filling her eyes.

'Goodnight, Dr Scott,' she said with exaggerated politeness.

With her head in the air she disappeared into her bedroom, only to lean against the closed door and put a hand to her mouth as it started to tremble.

Mother him!

How dared he? What woman in her right mind would want to merely mother a strong, handsome man like him? She strode across the room, pulling off her clothes as she went. Well, at least he had not accused her of other motives. Like not being able to resist wanting to see him again before she went to bed. Like wondering if seeing him again would help her to know if that fierce flare of attraction had been real or a fantasy. . .

She stilled. He had said something about not taking that kiss the wrong way. What way was she meant to take it? That it was only a moment of madness, a kiss of comfort? Perhaps it had started out that way for him but then she had let it get out of hand.

Somehow he must have guessed she had really just been waiting to see him again. To see if that feeling, that. . .that awareness would still be there between them.

Well, she'd had her answer to all of that!

She stomped across the room. In a few moments she had flung her clothes off, slipped into her nightdress and curled up in a tight ball on her bed.

So much for being worried about that horrible, irritating man when he'd had such a rough start in Coolong. So much for being worried about becoming too intimate with the new doctor in town. After all, she'd only met him that morning.

That morning! It seemed days ago!

A clenched fist thumped the pillow into a more comfortable mound. It didn't help.

She had been right the first time.

Give her tall-dark-and-handsome any day. Not an arrogant, handsome hunk with blond curls and eyes so blue that a woman could drown in them. . . And lips that set her heart on fire. And made her long for things that she had recently begun to realise might never be for her.

The anger began to fade. She tried to whip it up again. After all he had been horrible that morning, too, trying to put her in her place with his sarcasm.

But she had been very rude to him.

She screwed her eyes shut, trying to forget the fact that he could have made a lot more trouble for her with Bronwyn Brook. And he had been very nice to her this afternoon. Understanding her fears.

But he badly needed a haircut, she tried to convince herself. Those curls fell far too thickly behind his ears to rest on his shoulders. He was a *doctor* for goodness' sake. Doctors should have a short back and sides. Doctors should look. . .well. . .look more clinically tidy.

That thought banished the last of her indignation and anger. A self-derogatory grin tilted her lips.

There had been those moments at the hospital.

When he had tenderly stroked Brett's hair back with his large hand. When, at the same time, she had suddenly found herself wanting to reach out and run her fingers through Rowan's long ruffled curls. When she had wondered how they would feel springing around her fingers.

When he had looked at her. . .

She was most definitely attracted to him!

She bounced over in the bed but her undisciplined thoughts were impossible to control.

It had been a long, exhausting day and Kaycee at last fell asleep in the middle of thinking again about the touch and the taste of a man's lips. A man with blue eyes that had searched hers as though wanting to know all her secrets.

The next morning the shrill of the alarm drove her from her bed. Half-awake, she flung open the bathroom door and stumbled into a large firm body.

Arms closed around her and a low, startled chuckle brought her face up.

'Oh, I didn't dream you after all!' she beamed sleepily.

For a moment she relaxed and snuggled her head into the warmth of a soft neck. Her hands reached around to hold and mould bare, warm flesh. And warm muscles that rippled. . .and then quivered. . .

She froze.

Her mind cleared and she went to wrench herself away. Strong arms tightened around her. She muttered something incoherently. Then his hands slid to her shoulders and soft, warm lips slid across her mouth before he released her.

In a flash she was in the bathroom with the door slammed between them.

Oh, no! How to make a fool of yourself two mornings in a row!

After a few breathless moments she forced herself to start the shower. The running cold water didn't help. Vigorously towelling her body dry didn't help either. Then, when she had scrambled into her uniform, she paused and stared at the flushed, wild-eyed face looking back at her from the mirror.

How on earth was she going to face him over the breakfast table? What on earth could she say? Especially after his scathing words to her the night before!

But he *had* cuddled her for that brief, delicious moment.

To her utter relief the large kitchen was empty. It stayed empty while she swallowed a few mouthfuls of coffee and toast. There was still no sign of Rowan or her mother as she pulled the front door closed quietly behind her and hurried through the cool early morning breeze to her car.

Rowan heard Kaycee's car start up and knew that it was safe at last to venture out of his room. She had been a warm, cuddly bundle of temptation and a temptation that he had vowed only the night before to resist. But this morning, after a restless night, he had found her irresistible and the only way to control the desire to kiss her senseless had been to retreat to his room.

If she reacted to the thought of gossip around the town as strongly as she had intimated she would certainly hate them to become victims of gossip—as they undoubtedly would if they were caught kissing again!

As weary as he had been the night before, he had slept only fitfully. First there had been the image of Kaycee asleep on the lounge and his battle to keep his hands from touching her. Then there had been her angry, wounded expression. Then there was the small, valiant little boy, Brett, and then that other older boy's smashed-up body.

His hands clenched.

With an effort of will he forced his thoughts back to

Brett Porter. Despite his reassurances to his family he was still worried about the boy.

Rowan had given him three ampoules altogether—two polyvalent and the brown snake serum—before further supplies of antivenin had arrived from Newcastle by road just before dark. He had given one ampoule of the newly arrived brown snake antivenin to the smaller boy but now he wondered if he should have given more serum to both boys, remembering the experience of a friend of his.

He had been a doctor in a large country hospital and had thought his snake-bite victim was recovering well; had been just about to discharge him when he had suffered a severe brain haemorrhage and died. One thing his friend had apparently not done was follow-up blood chemistry and clotting-time tests.

But, of course, Rowan had been battling his own personal demons. Memories of Elle and his own child-hood and the nightmare that he had thought he had come to grips with and put behind him many years ago until he had seen those two kids in that old yellow car. . .

Now, should he have transferred the boys to Newcastle? This hospital did not even have an intensive care unit, just what they called a high dependency ward—although there wasn't too much equipment that it didn't have. They must have remained stable during the night or the staff would have contacted him.

He grabbed a quick breakfast, still forcing aside that old memory but not without a trace of fear that perhaps he had made a mistake deciding to get back into a country town. He was thankful that Mrs Wiseman had still not put in an appearance before he left the house.

When he passed the high school he checked the time.

It was not quite eight o'clock and he grinned slightly. Just as well! Best not to risk arriving too early to do a ward round. Might get bowled over by a belligerent nurse pushing a wheelchair!

Then he sobered, remembering the old man in that chair. Perhaps he should have told Kaycee about his collapse last night. Apparently he was an old family friend. There had been no chance the night before and then this morning. . .

The memory of a soft, sleepy body slipping into his arms as though it belonged there pulsated through him. Annoyed with himself, he swung a little too fast into the hospital grounds and his tyres protested with a squeal.

Kaycee had been immensely relieved when she had arrived that morning, meticulously on time and spick and span, to find that Sister Bronwyn Brook had three days off. Hopefully she would have forgotten all about Kaycee's bad Sunday when she returned.

She even dared to pop in to see Brett and Stevie while her patients were finishing their breakfast and was talking to Shirley Porter in the high dependency ward when Rowan entered the room. He paused when he saw her and then his eyes twinkled devilishly and his lips tilted.

Kaycee's heart lurched. Why did the man have to be so darned attractive?

A wave of hot embarrassment swept through her. A constant state near this man, she thought angrily. She had been dreading this meeting; had even hoped to avoid him altogether while on duty.

Mrs Porter was looking curiously from her to the doctor. Kaycee's voice had faltered to a stop in the middle of what she was saying. She looked down at the small boy in the bed, trying to get herself under control and not rush out of the room.

'Good morning, Mrs Porter. Kaycee. Hi, boys.'

The heat in Kaycee's face intensified at the calm, professional tone of his voice. Keeping her face averted, she murmured a greeting as he advanced to Brett's bed and picked up the bundle of charts hooked over the end rail.

Despite the fact that he had obviously only been highly amused by their early morning encounter Kaycee was relieved to see him. While she had been quietly talking to the boys' mother she had been taking note of Brett and becoming rather worried about him.

Both boys still had their IV cannulas in but only the drip was still running slowly into Brett, apparently to counteract some dehydration. Whereas Stevie was rather irritable, but obviously rather enjoying all the fuss, Kaycee had noted that Brett was very drowsy and quiet. Of course, it could just be the effects of the medication he was on. She had peeped at his medication chart and noted that he was being given valium as a muscle relaxant, as well as the cortisone that was routinely given for a week after the serum.

As she had greeted his mother and smiled at him Brett had opened his eyes and squinted up briefly at her. But there had been no change of expression on his face. He had opened his mouth and tried to say something when his mother had offered him a drink. Frustrated, he had ended up shaking his head very slightly and turning away from them.

There was also a small bloodstain on the bandage protecting his second cannula and the white dressing over the bite sites also looked moist.

Mrs Porter had told her that blood samples had been taken again that morning to determine any chemical imbalance and how much the blood-clotting mechanism had been damaged.

Kaycee took a deep breath and said clearly, 'Brett doesn't want to talk to us today.'

Rowan turned his head towards her sharply. She held his eyes and added meaningfully, 'He didn't want to swallow a drink either.'

'I think he's probably just fed up with me fussing.' There was a strained note in Mrs Porter's voice as she managed a slight smile.

She's been getting worried too, Kaycee realised. 'I. . .I must get back to my patients and see if anyone needs more help with their breakfast.' Kaycee was rather proud of the fact that there wasn't the slightest tremor in her voice. 'I'll try and see you again when I finish work, boys.'

She forced a bright smile at their still-curious mother and turned to flee.

'Just a moment, Kaycee. Are you working here in High Dependency with these boys?'

She risked a glance at him. He was still studying the bundle of observation charts in his hands. When he looked up at her she saw a frown on his face.

'No, I'm still rostered in the wards where I was yesterday,' she said quietly.

He hesitated.

'Something wrong?'

'Would you mind asking the RN in charge if I could. . .?' He broke off as Sister Allen bustled into the room. His voice sharpened with authority as he continued 'Ah, there you are, Sister. Thank you, Kaycee, I won't hold you up after all. Would you mind

telling your mother I should be home for tea tonight?'
he added smoothly, and then moved towards Sister
Allen and out of hearing of his patients and their
mother.

As Kaycee started thankfully towards the door the
RN glared at her disapprovingly. Kaycee wasn't sure
if it was because of Dr Scott's last comment or the fact
that she had not asked permission to visit patients under
Sister Allen's jurisdiction.

As she reached the doorway Kaycee heard Rowan's
lowered voice become even crisper and colder. 'Sister
Allen, could you please explain why this head injury
observation chart has not been filled in since five a.m.?
It's imperative we pick up any neurological changes
immediately. These boys must be nursed as for head
injuries in case of cranial nerve or haemorrhage damage. Brett, especially, must be awakened and examined
at least hourly! And has a urine test for blood been
attended to this morning? We must also pick up
immediately any sign of kidney damage!'

Kaycee winced as she raced out of earshot. He
sounded very cross and she was glad that she wasn't
responsible. She felt sympathy for Sister if she had
changed the frequency of the neurological observations
he had requested. Without a resident hospital doctor
sometimes the senior nursing staff did change those
kind of orders. But this was not a doctor whose orders
should be tampered with in any way!

CHAPTER SEVEN

'SISTER, I do appreciate the fact that the boys had been disturbed all night with the regular observations but in this case I expected my instructions to be carried out without change!'

Rowan was extremely annoyed and more with himself than with Sister Allen and her staff. He had forgotten last night that this was a country hospital with more flexibility for the nursing staff to make decisions. He should have spelt out more clearly just why keeping up the frequent observations on Brett was so important. Going by Sister Allen's furious face she thought so, too.

'Has the blood pathology been done yet?' he asked in a tightly controlled voice. He had signed the appropriate order forms before going home the night before but perhaps he should have spelt out how urgent they were too!

'Yes, Doctor,' Sister Allen snapped coldly. 'As early as possible.' She thrust a sheet of paper at him. 'The results. Phoned through a moment ago.'

He took them without comment, deliberately ignoring the triumphant gleam in her eye. What did the woman want? A medal?

Then he relented, remembering that he had been warned the previous day that all pathology had to be done by a visiting pathologist from Taree. He had hoped that his horror had not been too evident to the staff who seemed to be waiting for his reaction to a further reminder that he no longer worked in a large city hospital with all its conveniences.

'You must have contacted the pathologist very early, Sister. Thank you very much.' He smiled slightly at her. 'I didn't think we would have the results quite so soon.'

He noticed her relax slightly as she told him, 'It was phoned through immediately. We won't get the written report until later.'

Rowan studied the report carefully. His heart sank and he looked up at her again.

Before he could speak she said crisply, 'More antivenin?'

He nodded. 'I'm afraid so, Sister.'

'What about transferring him to Newcastle?'

Rowan said hesitantly, 'I know we don't have all the equipment we should but I don't want to do that unless absolutely necessary. One of the parents would have to go and one stay here with Stevie. It's always very difficult for parents being so far from home. Let's see how he responds to more serum first. Do you have enough staff for someone to stay with him?'

'As long as enrolled nurses like your friend, Nurse Wiseman, stay on their own wards and aren't distracted I'm sure the DON will allocate another nurse from those already on duty, Doctor.'

Before Rowan could respond the sister bustled past him. He looked after her thoughtfully. There had been a sharp, disapproving tone in her voice. His heart sank. Obviously the hospital grapevine was flourishing here even faster than at his last hospital. He and Kaycee were already an object of gossip and he knew how much that was going to upset her.

*　　*　　*

Kaycee had to force herself to focus her attention on the patients allotted to her care after the encounter with Rowan. She couldn't get the man out of her head. Mechanically she finished the showers and bed-making, took and charted the fourth-hourly observations and was more than usually thankful when it was her turn for the morning tea-break.

There were a couple of other nurses already in the staff-room. They broke off their conversation a little abruptly when they saw Kaycee. Although she had worked with them quite often she had never been particularly friendly with them but was still a little disconcerted when they barely acknowledged her greeting, finished their drinks and left rather abruptly.

Then she shrugged as others arrived and greeted her cheerfully, teasing her about her rescue of the snake-bite victims.

Then the nurse from Accident and Emergency arrived. She nodded briefly in acknowledgement of the murmur of greetings and went to fetch her hot drink. As she joined them at the table she asked quietly, 'Anyone happen to know that young motorbike rider?'

Everyone sobered quickly. There were a few shakes of the head.

Kaycee looked from one to the other. 'What motorbike rider?'

'The one brought in last night. Died shortly after admission.' The nurse's voice was curt.

Kaycee's mind tumbled. She had decided this morning when told about Ken Rodgers's condition that Rowan had been upset about that. But this was far, far worse.

With increasing comprehension of Rowan's grimness the night before she said anxiously, 'None of the staff in Surg and Med have said anything. I know a few of the lads around town who own bikes. Who was it?'

'Perhaps they thought you already knew. Didn't Dr Scott tell you, Kaycee?'

To her annoyance Kaycee felt the flush of embarrassment as all eyes focused on her. 'Why should he?' She stared back steadily.

'He's living with you, isn't he?'

Several eyes widened and swung towards Kaycee but before Kaycee could say anything the nurse continued sadly, 'Apparently he was very upset last night but they were saying this morning that there was absolutely nothing anyone could have done.'

'What do you mean? What happened?' Kaycee asked huskily, thinking of the exhausted, angry man who had confronted her last night.

'Eighteen-year-old ran his bike into a tree on his family's farm. No helmet. Massive head injuries. Died shortly after arrival.' The words were clipped.

Kaycee caught her breath. Eighteen. 'Who was it?' The nurse told her and she put one hand up to her mouth. 'He went to school with Drew. Was even at his party Saturday night.'

She did not add that he had been one of the teenagers who had sneered when he'd found out that there was no beer there.

She stood up slowly. 'I should make sure Mum knows so she can ring Drew. He wasn't a particularly close friend but he'll still be very upset.'

Kaycee wondered briefly why Rowan had not told her about the teenager. Then she remembered the bleakness in his eyes, not quite disguised by his anger. He had taken some of his anger and feeling of helplessness out on her. The only way to survive the horror was to try and block out the memory of a smashed body and distraught parents.

She, too, had never been able to talk to anyone outside the hospital about some of the sad things that had taunted her over the years.

Then she caught her breath as she remembered the expression in his face after her comment about staying up for him. A mother last night would have waited in vain for her son.

But why had none of the staff that morning mentioned the accident to her? Perhaps, like the nurse from Emergency, they thought she would know. Perhaps they had been too dismayed by the deterioration in Ken Rodgers. When she had heard that report she had felt a little peeved that Rowan had not told her about their old family friend. He had been transferred to High Dependency during the night and again put on continuous oxygen and IV antibiotics. Now he was improving rapidly.

By midday the news of the young local teenager's death had swept through the hospital to staff, patients and visitors alike. Kaycee rang her mother from the public phone on her way to lunch.

'Oh, Kaycee,' her mother whispered sadly, 'that family was among your father's first patients. He probably attended that boy's birth.'

And that's what a small town does, too, Kaycee thought as she hurried off to the dining-room to snatch a quick meal. Everyone knows everyone else and so everyone grieves.

And yet, she thought unexpectedly, there's a kind of comfort in that.

Just as it was when Dad died, she suddenly acknowledged. At the time she had dismissed the sympathy and offers of support as hypocritical. But now, with added maturity, she saw that the majority had been genuine and of great benefit to them as a family.

'Did you hear that one of your pet kids isn't too good, Kaycee?' a nurse asked as she sat across from her.

To Kaycee's dismay she went on to tell her that the paralysis of Brett's muscles had worsened and it had been necessary to intubate and place him on a respirator. The anti-coagulant in the snake venom was also causing haemoglobin to show up in his urine tests. He was being given another ampoule of monovalent brown snake serum and might need more.

Kaycees mouth went dry. 'So, are we going to keep him or. . .?'

The nurse shrugged. 'Doc rang to enquire about the copter to transfer him to Newcastle. But apparently there's a dense fog over the mountains and it's not expected to clear for some time. The fog also means that an ambulance trip would be far too slow. Sister said they'll see what happens after this extra antivenin.'

Kaycee had to race back to the ward then and was far too busy with her own patients to visit Brett again. But she found her thoughts straying so often to a tall, blond man and the decisions he would have to make for his little patient that she was very thankful that the rest of her shift went smoothly.

Monday afternoon was admission day for Theatre cases scheduled for the following morning. For the last hour of her shift Kaycee was kept busy filling out charts and forms and settling in a sad young woman scheduled for a hysterectomy and a very nervous middle-aged man who would arrive back in the ward minus his gall bladder.

'Never been in hospital before,' Jim Newton boasted. He gave a nervous twitter. 'Just my luck to cop a new bloke on his first operating day.'

'Oh, I don't know,' Kaycee said mildly as she wrapped the cloth cover of the sphygmomanometer around his arm to take his blood pressure. 'I think you're very fortunate to have timed your operation so well. Dr Scott was a surgeon in a very well-known and highly thought-of hospital in Sydney. You can be sure they would only employ someone who was very competent.'

She finished putting the stethoscope earpieces in place as she was speaking and commenced inflating the cuff. Mr Newton looked over her shoulder towards the doorway. She thought that his glance was only at the other nurse on duty until a deep voice with a hint of laughter in it spoke behind her after she'd finished the reading and removed the stethoscope.

'Thank you for the vote of confidence, Nurse Wiseman. Good afternoon, Mr Newton.'

I hope I'm not destined to spend my time near him in a perpetual state of embarrassment, she thought savagely as she managed to smile blandly back at him for Jim Newton's sake. She hoped that he couldn't see the way her pen shook as she recorded the blood pressure reading that she had just taken.

Then she looked up suddenly. 'Brett!' she exclaimed fearfully. 'He. . .'

Rowan was smiling and she had her answer even before he spoke. 'Doing much better, thank God. We've decided not to order that helicopter.'

Kaycee beamed back at him.

'That the kid bitten by a King Brown snake?'

They both turned and stared at the man. Typical,

thought Kaycee crossly, the town's gossip not getting it quite right.

Rowan frowned. 'He wasn't bitten by a King Brown. They were baby common or Eastern brown snakes.'

'There,' Jim Newton said with considerable satisfaction. 'Told the missus it couldn't have been a King Brown. Not in the Hunter Valley. Most people over the years who reckon they've seen one have probably seen large ordinary brown snakes.'

'Nothing ordinary about the Eastern brown snake,' Rowan said firmly. 'It's the second most venomous snake, in order of lethal potency, in the world. Fortunately it doesn't produce as much venom as a taipan or even a King Brown or. . .'

He broke off. He looked across at Kaycee. Their eyes acknowledged what he had almost said out loud— or Brett might not have survived.

Kaycee shuddered. As it was those multiple bites had apparently given him more poison than they had first thought possible. Or some of the bites had occurred well before she'd found the boys.

'He's a lucky kid, all right. Heard that one of the nurses from here found him,' Mr Newton murmured.

Kaycee flashed a look at Rowan. He grinned at her.

'Yeah,' he drawled. 'Did an excellent job, she did.'

A dart of delight shot through her but she scowled at him with a warning look that plainly said, don't you dare tell him!

Fortunately their patient did not see the exchange above him as he continued, 'I've worked in the forests around the Barrington Tops all my life. Some years back a bush walker wasn't so fortunate. One of my mates found him dead on a track. Silly mug, going out there by himself. My mate reckoned there were an

awful lot of bites on his leg. Tiger snake, they reckoned.
He. . .'

Kaycee felt sick. If she had not gone down to the
creek. . . If she had gone into the house instead. . .

'Right, Mr Newton, that's enough about snakes.
Those of us brought up on a farm are a bit more used
to them than Nurse here is, I suspect.' Rowan interrupted. He moved abruptly and flung back the man's
bedclothes. 'I'm sure you have plenty of other work to
attend to Nurse. I can manage here.'

Kaycee, still feeling rather shocked, stared blankly
for a moment. Why was he snapping at her again? Then
he swung around and his eyes flashed a message of
sympathy and understanding at her.

She gulped, murmured, 'Certainly, Doctor,' and
thankfully escaped.

Kaycee managed to keep very busy after that and it
wasn't until she was on her way home that she allowed
herself to think about that understanding and sympathy
in a man who only the day before had been a complete
stranger. He had an uncanny way of knowing what she
was feeling.

Once again she found herself wishing she knew more
about him and pulled a face. As bad as all the other
gossips! But that still did not stop her brooding for a
while on the snippet of information that Rowan had
been brought up on a farm.

Suddenly she wondered if that was one of the reasons
that he was working here. Had the faster pace and
bright lights of city life begun to pall? She shook her
head. Surely not after all the years he must have spent
doing his training. And, then, to reach the position of
surgical registrar took several years after graduating.

Even if it all did eventually pall I would still like the

opportunity to see for myself what those bright lights and pace are like, she thought wistfully. There would be so many opportunities for art exhibitions, theatre shows and, above all, arts and crafts lessons.

Suddenly she felt a chill. The rumour around was that whoever did the locum work for Dr Gordon was really on trial about coming in to replace him when he retired in the near future.

Last night she had made up her mind that as soon as the house was sold, if not before, she would make the transition to the city. If Rowan was intending to move to the country it would mean that they would rarely, if ever, see each other.

And then she impatiently wondered why that thought should dismay her so much.

By evening Rowan felt so weary that he wondered how much longer he could keep working. Meal breaks had been scarce all day as constant demands were made on his time. This town did not need a three-doctor practice; it needed six, at least!

He was just suturing up a sliced finger when a tall, handsome man with a neat moustache strolled into the emergency department. The sister glanced up and greeted him briefly before bending over her paperwork again. Out of the corner of his eye Rowan saw the man glancing casually around at the now-empty cubicles as he came towards him.

'Dr Scott? Glad it's nice and quiet for you on your first day. A bit different from your big city hospital, isn't it?'

Rowan glanced up at him for a moment. This could only be Dr Swain. He did not like the gleam in the man's eyes and the tone of voice one bit. His heart sank and anger stirred in him.

Steady, Scott, don't get into a fight on your first day with one of the partners.

He bent over the finger again, finished tying the last suture, snipped off the thread and said quietly to the rather pale woman, 'I'll get Sister to spray this and put on a protective dressing. And she'll give you an antitetanus injection. Try to keep it as dry as possible and come back in a week to have the stitches out.'

Then he straightened and looked back at the handsome face, now frowning slightly at being ignored.

'As a matter of fact we've been very busy today,' Rowan said evenly. 'And yesterday, too.'

He moved into the treatment room and started to wash his hands. The man hesitated and then followed him. Rowan tore off a generous piece of paper towelling. As he dried his hands thoroughly he studied the man.

For a place that apparently thrived on gossip there had been no comment in his presence on this man's unexpected absence for two days. Only the formidable Sister Allen had dropped her guard and scowled when she had heard him ringing the surgery to see if there had been any word from this man.

'I take it you must be Dr John Swain. I trust your family problems have now been sorted out satisfactorily?' For the life of him Rowan could not prevent the sarcasm creeping into his voice.

Dr Swain's eyes narrowed slightly and then he grinned knowingly. 'Very satisfactorily, in fact.'

'I'm pleased about that. I'm sure Dr Gordon will also be glad to hear that your. . .er—mother, was it?—

is no longer in need of her son's attention.' Rowan looked at him steadily.

He felt a measure of satisfaction as the man lost his self-confident air and alarm flashed across his face. 'Oh, I'm sure there's no need to bother Dr Gordon with such a small matter. I'm sure——.'

'And I'm sure—*very* sure in fact—that Dr Gordon would want to be informed that this town was left for several hours without any doctor at all on call. It was fortunate I was not delayed any more than I was!'

'But you were delayed, Doctor, and you can hardly blame me if——'

'I do blame you, Doctor!' Rowan allowed the fury that he could feel building up in him to flare out. Then he checked himself. He lowered his voice. 'I was not scheduled to commence work until this morning and then only after being shown around by you. And if I had not been here how would you have been able to explain the death of two small boys from snake bite and no doctor in attendance when a fatal accident victim was brought here late last night?'

John Swain lost colour. Horror filled his face. He swallowed and opened his mouth but Rowan had had enough.

'When I finish writing up this last case, Doctor, I'm going home.' He unclipped the pager from his belt, picked up the other man's hand and slammed it into it. 'It's all yours. I'll be unavailable until eight tomorrow morning for the theatre cases.'

'But. . .but you were rostered to be on call tonight, and I——'

'And you were rostered to be on call until nine this morning!'

Rowan turned and made his way to the desk. He grabbed the last patient's card.

'But, Rowan, old man, you don't understand. I had an important appointment this evening. . .'

Rowan did not bother to look up as he scribbled furiously. He signed his name and handed the card to the waiting nurse.

'Sister, I'm off duty until tomorrow. Dr Swain has just taken over. Would you let the staff in the wards know?'

He looked steadily at the sister who was glancing from one doctor to the other.

'Certainly, Dr Scott,' she murmured, and he heard the amusement and. . .and, yes, satisfaction in her voice.

As he swung around and made for the door she said sharply, 'Dr Swain, Medical have been waiting ages for medications to be recharted and. . .'

Rowan was home in plenty of time for tea that night. However, he was very quiet and Kaycee could see how exhausted he was. She wasn't sure if she was relieved or not when he excused himself immediately after the meal.

'I need to finish unpacking and sort my things out,' he murmured abruptly and wished them both goodnight.

She ended up seeing very little of him for several days. So much so that Kaycee began to wonder if he was avoiding her. She did see him briefly at work when he visited her post-op patients but he put on such a professional mantle that she was taken back. There were no more exchanged glances or personal communications between them.

In many ways it was a relief for Kaycee that when Bronwyn Brooks was on duty she did every round of patients with him, including those that she had allocated to Kaycee. It was obvious to all the staff that Bronwyn Brooks was seriously smitten with the handsome new doctor.

By the time Rowan had been there a few weeks Kaycee was a bundle of contradictory, confused feelings. At home they mainly encountered each other at mealtimes when their rosters allowed. He had very quickly become a real favourite with her mother. But, although he was unfailingly friendly and polite with Kaycee, he maintained a certain distance from her that she found increasingly difficult to convince herself she did not mind in the least.

At work he continued to be very formal, even abrupt, whenever he needed to speak to her. He, more than once, made it abundantly clear to her that all communication between them at the hospital was to be strictly professional and in no way would he discuss their work at home.

Obviously he had decided, as she reluctantly had, that kissing her had been a mistake that would not be repeated. But he could at least be as friendly with me as he is with the rest of the staff, she thought indignantly a few times. There was no need to snap her head off for the least little thing! After all it had been he who had grabbed and kissed her on that very first day.

His attitude to her did not improve; if anything it became worse. The tension between them at work increased and Kaycee knew that speculation was rife about them. Her indignation gradually gave way to sheer bewilderment and deepening anger and hurt.

Why, when everyone else raved about his competence and his patience with patients and staff alike, did he treat her so differently?

She found out the reason, or thought she had, at the end of an evening shift.

For once the patients had settled early. Her work now finished, Kaycee was in the staff-room making cups of coffee while they waited for the night staff to come on duty.

Jill Lawe had been on her annual holiday. Kaycee had seen her a few times and had even had coffee with her one morning when they had met while shopping. Kaycee knew that tonight would be her first night back. When Jill entered the staff-room Kaycee greeted her with a welcoming smile. However, there was no answering friendliness on Jill's face.

'Well, I think you could have told me, Kaycee,' Jill greeted her sharply. 'I thought we were good friends!'

'And good evening to you, too, Jill,' Kaycee said cheerfully. 'And told you what?'

'About your boyfriend, of course!'

Kaycee swung around so sharply that the cup of coffee slopped over onto her hand.

'Ouch!' She put down the cup with a thud. 'Now look what you've made me do. And what on earth are you talking about?' she added crossly as she wiped her stinging hand. 'What boyfriend?'

'The one you're having an affair with, of course. Our Dr Rowan Scott. No one's being fooled a scrap by your coldness to each other on duty. You could at least have told me how well you knew him that first day. Even if you didn't want to admit to an affair with him!'

CHAPTER EIGHT

'WHAT did you say?'

Jill narrowed her eyes. 'Why so surprised? Think nobody would find out?' She snorted. 'You need to be a bit more discreet about kissing him and having him boarding at your place if it was such a big secret!'

Kaycee stared at her. She closed her eyes for a moment. This must be a dream. Why on earth would Jill, of all people, be saying these crazy. . .stupid things?

She opened her eyes. Jill had her back to her, busily putting a teabag in a cup.

'Jill, are you telling me you think I'm having. . .having an affair with Rowan Scott?'

Jill sniffed huffily.

'It's not true!' Kaycee heard her voice start to rise and fought for control. 'Where on earth did you hear such crazy nonsense?'

Jill turned and studied her face for a moment. A flicker of doubt crossed her face. 'You mean you're not?'

'Of course I'm not,' Kaycee denied furiously. 'I only met the man a few weeks ago!'

'That's not what people are saying.'

'Of course I did!' She swallowed on a tide of fury. 'People? What people?'

Jill shrugged. 'Everyone I've talked to. You already knew each other that first morning. He even knew your taste in music, for goodness' sake! Apparently he even went to your brother's birthday party.'

Suddenly Kaycee swore. And swore loudly.

Jill gaped at her. 'Kaycee! I've never ever heard you swear before!'

'And it may not be the last time!' Kaycee said through gritted teeth. 'It's this da. . .this town, isn't it? When they can't gossip about something that has happened they make it up!'

'You hate this town, don't you, Kaycee?' Sympathy filled Jill's face. 'Ever since. . .ever since all that talk about your mother and father. . .' She stopped as Kaycee spun away.

There was silence for a moment. 'None of that rubbish was true either. I'm sure it wasn't. Dad loved Mum far too much to ever. . .to ever. . .' Kaycee's voice choked, filled with bitterness. 'But Dad was very hurt. I. . .I always thought it hastened that last heart attack.'

Kaycee swung around. 'But rumours like this can hurt a doctor. Even such a well-known GP as Dad.' She took a deep, shuddering breath. 'Especially someone new to the town. No wonder Rowan's hardly been speaking to me. Probably thinks I started the gossip!' She looked helplessly across at Jill. 'Jill, how did this rumour start? What exactly have you heard?'

Kaycee forced herself to drive home safely. She didn't bother parking the car in the garage. Her car door was slammed as it never had been in all the long years of its life and she flew into the house, letting the front door slam behind her also.

It was almost midnight. Normally she would have been home over half an hour before. But, as could often happen on a smooth shift, the evening staff had been collecting their belongings to go home after reporting to the night staff when an emergency had occurred.

One of the elderly patients had tried to get out of bed unassisted, fallen heavily and possibly fractured her pelvis. At the same time a couple of other patients had begun demanding urgent attention. So the nurses going off duty had shrugged and stayed to help until the night staff could cope.

Fortunately Rowan had not been on call. Kaycee wasn't quite sure if it was fortunate for her sake or his!

Through all the furore Kaycee's hurt and anger had not diminished. She wasn't sure with whom she was the angriest—the town, herself for allowing things to happen or. . .or this man who had come and was disrupting her life!

On the quiet drive home she'd had more time to dwell on it all. In more ways than one this man was disrupting her life. At first she had been excited but now. . . Anger built up into unreasonable fury.

She was trembling with it as she stopped outside Rowan's door and raised her fist to pound on it. It flew open before her hand landed. The big, bare-chested man with tousled hair and a half-awake, anxious expression came barrelling out.

'Kaycee! What's wrong? Have you had an accident?'

'No! Yes! You're my accident!'

Two large, now-familiar hands reached out to clasp her shoulders. She was too worked up to take any notice of the confused, worried look on his face.

'And don't touch me!' she yelled even louder.

He was far too close. She twisted and tried to wrench out of his grasp. His grip tightened. It suddenly felt very familiar. Her rage increased and her hands came up to slam into his chest.

'Kaycee, calm down!'

'You come into my life. You let the staff think we know each other. Even Mr Rodgers thought we must know each other! You bundle me into your car. You kiss me. . .right where that old tent-hire gossip saw us. And his wife would work in the kitchen, wouldn't she? It's not enough that they should spread rotten rumours about my mother and father. Now the whole town's gossiping about me. . .us. . .you. . .you horrible man!'

Another clenched fist slammed into his shoulder and then the furious tears began streaming down her face.

She barely registered the absolute shock on his face or that his hands dropped away from her at last to let other arms enfold Kaycee and draw her away. A soft voice murmured comfort as it used to when she was a small girl with a grazed knee. Before the world had become such a harsh, cruel place.

'Oh, Mum, the gossip! I hate it all! I hate it!'

'Yes, darling, I know. I know. Hush now, everything will be all right. You're worn out. It's not Rowan's fault.'

Kaycee let her mother lead her into her bedroom. She didn't see the look exchanged between Rowan and the sad-faced Cathryn Wiseman as she attempted to smile reassuringly at the pale, stern-faced man.

Kaycee cried all the tears she should have shed holding onto her mother years ago. When the torrent had subsided she pushed herself away and sat looking down at her clenched hands.

'Gossip can be hurtful, even deadly, to hopes and dreams, Kaycee.'

Kaycee looked up. Her mother was very pale but she gazed steadily back at her daughter.

'But it can only do real damage when people who should know better believe it.' Mrs Wiseman's lips quivered for a moment and then she tilted her chin. 'Your father *never* believed those wicked lies about me, Kaycee. He knew they were the fabrication of a sick mind. . .a very jealous mind. Unfortunately. . .'

She paused and a tormented look crept into the brown eyes that were so like Kaycee's. 'Unfortunately,' she continued in a whisper, 'I at first believed the wicked lies the same clever woman told me about him. That lack of trust upset him very much.'

Kaycee stared at her through a mist. 'The. . .the story about you having an affair wasn't. . .wasn't true?'

A flash of anger brought a trace of colour to the pale cheeks. 'Ah, so you did hear that rumour. I've often wondered. . . Kaycee, how could you not know that the only man I ever even saw was your father? Thank God he knew that! The. . .the friends I've had since he died have been only that—friends—because I was just. . .just so lonely. . .'

Anguish rushed through Kaycee in a fresh wave. All these years she had not known what to believe; had even half believed the lie. She had grieved so much for her father; had been secretly angry with both of her parents. Her father for leaving them. And her mother. . .

She had let it all fester and cause the wall that had sprung up between her and her mother—the wall that had grown so thick and apparently impenetrable that Kaycee had only wanted to get away. But there had been Andrew and. . .

'Is that why you were so sick during those years, Mum? Because. . .because you hadn't trusted Dad?'

Mrs Wiseman's lips twisted in a wry grimace as she looked down at their clasped hands. 'Well, I've been told my asthma is partly caused by allergies but during those years it was definitely mostly because of stress.

It ate into me. I. . .I've been so much better since I
met Bob.'

Her face softened. She glanced up at Kaycee. There
was wonder in her face. 'Bob. . . Bob loves me—really
loves me—no matter how weak and stupid I am. It's
been so hard to forgive myself. Your father died thinking I still believed the gossip about him. For a long
time I couldn't sleep; couldn't concentrate. Nothing
seemed to matter any more. And when I started to come
out of all that there was another pressure.'

She hesitated, looking at Kaycee uncertainly.

'It was me, wasn't it?' Kaycee took a shuddering
breath. 'I had taken over. Wouldn't let you make
decisions.'

'I don't think I was capable of making decisions for
a long time. Even. . .even now, Bob keeps telling me
to have more confidence in myself. Besides getting
married and going to live with Bob, the main reason I
decided to sell the house was to make you see I'm
different now and to. . .to set you free to go and be and
do what you really want to.

'You. . . All these years you've worried me. I knew
you wanted to go to Newcastle or Sydney to do your
RN training but I just wasn't coping with life at all for
such a long time and I. . .I couldn't bear to talk about
it at first. You were so young.

'And then the years seemed to just slip by and you
were settled here. I was never sure how much you had
heard and it was so hard to talk to you. And I've been
too much of a coward too long. And. . .and the whole
miserable business was so painful for so long.'

The words had poured out in a relieved stream. The
two women stared at each other but neither were prepared for the angry voice from the doorway.

'No wonder you couldn't talk if your daughter explodes very often into a fury like she did tonight.'

Both women swung around. Kaycee stared blankly at the tall man.

'Forget about me?' he said in the gentle voice he used when he was absolutely furious.

Kaycee opened her mouth but, before she could get a word out, her mother stood up.

'Dr Scott, have you been listening to our very private conversation?'

'No, of course not,' he snapped. 'Only your last statement. But how long was I supposed to wait in the corridor to find out what on earth's the matter with her?'

'Do I need to remind you that you are not a guest in this house but a boarder?' Mrs Wiseman's quiet, dignified voice rang with authority and the mother-voice protecting her child. 'And how dare you comment on something you know nothing about?'

For the first time Kaycee saw dynamic Rowan Scott momentarily disconcerted.

Kaycee looked at her mother with new eyes. Suddenly she realised how gradually her mother had been changing since she had started going out with Bob Gould. Now she realised with the eyes of maturity, as never before, just how much her mother had collapsed mentally as well as physically after the sudden death of her husband. For years she had seemed only too willing to allow her daughter to make decisions; to run the house.

Kaycee winced. Her own attitude had been so hard, so managing, that the few timid attempts her mother had made to do things she had scornfully squashed. Perhaps she should have not been so astonished when her mother had done so well at that first-aid course last year. Now she was taking the reins of the family back into her hands with a vengeance.

'You didn't close the door and I was worried about Kaycee.' Rowan had straightened at Mrs Wiseman's words but his eyes were searching Kaycee's tear-streaked face. 'I would apologise but it's not every day either that a little wildcat attacks a boarder for no apparent reason.'

'I apologise for my daughter, Dr Scott. However, she had a very good reason but she's too upset and exhausted for lengthy explanations now.' Mrs Wiseman moved between him and Kaycee, an impressive figure despite her dressing gown and sleep-tousled hair.

'No matter what has happened in the past there's no excuse for her behaviour tonight and I want to know what's happened!'

Mrs Wiseman's voice cracked across his angry words. 'You don't need to know tonight! Tomorrow will be time enough.'

Kaycee stood up and moved towards them. 'I'm all right, Mum. I can—'

Mrs Wiseman rounded on her. 'No, you're not all right, Kaycee. Words can be said when you're both angry and exhausted that can never be taken back and which later you may both regret.' Her voice deepened as she added fervently, 'I know that only too well.'

Kaycee stared at her mother wordlessly. She could hardly remember a time when her mother had been so forceful and determined. Then she looked past her to Rowan. There was a flood of colour high on that even more forceful man's face. His cheek-bones seemed more prominent; his jawline was rigid as he controlled his fury.

A wave of regret and weariness swept through her. 'I'm. . .I'm sorry, Rowan—' she began in a choked voice but her mother swept in again.

'Of course you are but no more tonight.'

The glitter in Rowan's eyes dimmed a little. He nodded abruptly. 'But I do expect an explanation. What shift are you on tomorrow?'

'A morning shift,' she answered wearily and glanced at her watch.

'I know,' her mother snapped, 'and you will be lucky to get five hours' sleep. Rotten quick shifts! I don't know why nurses' rosters have to be still in the Dark Ages.'

A gleam of amusement completely changed the grim expression on Rowan's face. Kaycee met his eyes with an answering glimmer of understanding. Both knew that there were times in a doctor's life when he didn't even get those precious few hours' sleep.

He held her gaze, all amusement fading away. 'We have to talk, Kaycee. As soon as possible.'

Kaycee nodded. 'Yes,' she answered as quietly as he had spoken. 'You've heard the rumours?'

He nodded abruptly but before he could speak Mrs Wiseman said crossly, 'Now, that's enough. Out!'

Rowan hesitated again and then he suddenly smiled charmingly in defeat, nodded and disappeared.

Kaycee looked at her mother with respect. Not many people over the years would have been able to order that dynamic man around and get away with it.

But the next day there was no opportunity for them to talk and the days following that proved to be just as frustrating. Then the days gradually stretched to weeks,

with Kaycee miserably deciding that Rowan had
changed his mind about their need to talk. She knew
that he had spoken to her mother but did not know
what had been said. She came to the unwelcome con-
clusion that he had decided to put the whole miserable
night behind him as not important enough to
mention again.

But the pressure of work at the hospital continued
almost unabated. Ian Taylor had returned for several
days, only to receive word of his father's death. So
once more Rowan and John Swain had been left to
cope. Rowan's few off-duty hours rarely coincided
with Kaycee's, so much so that she even wondered if
that was at times contrived.

However, Rowan and Kaycee saw each other briefly
in the wards. For Kaycee those moments brought very
mixed feelings. She found herself increasingly looking
forward to even those contacts with him but they often
only led to more embarrassment and increasing apprehension.

Rowan's attitude to her had changed. At least in
front of the staff at the hospital. Now he smiled warmly
at her and greeted her so familiarly that Kaycee could
have thrown something at him. Perversely she wished
that he had remained as taciturn and unfriendly as
before. All it was doing was fuelling the gossip and
causing Bronwyn Brooks to be even more unpleasant.

Kaycee had begun to think that she might be
desperate enough to write a letter to him demanding
that he refute the rumours, not give them more fuel!
Better still, she hoped that the real estate agent would
find somewhere for him to rent, even if it was only for
the remainder of his time in Coolong.

Then, one morning, Bronwyn Brooks was off duty

and one of Kaycee's allocated patients needed an IV drip relocated. The RNs were frantically busy and only too happy for Kaycee to organise it. Fortunately Rowan was already in the hospital when she went to ring him.

Being only a forty-bed hospital, the sister in charge of Emergency was also in charge of Maternity and the small high dependency unit. Kaycee groaned silently when she heard Sister Allen's abrupt voice answer the phone in Maternity.

'Could I speak to Dr Scott please, Sister?' Kaycee asked politely.

'No, you can't, Nurse Wiseman,' Sister Allen snapped. 'And you should know better than to make personal calls to him on duty.'

The phone went dead. Kaycee took the phone receiver away from her ear and stared at it.

This had gone too far!

She dialled the number again with trembling fingers. When Sister Allen's voice sounded again Kaycee took a deep breath and snapped angrily, 'Sister Allen, would you inform Dr Scott that Mrs Wilde's IV cannula has gone into the tissues and needs resisting as soon as possible.'

There was dead silence for a moment. When the sister spoke her voice was only a little milder. 'My apologies, Nurse. I'll tell him but I'm afraid we've had a. . .a difficult time here and he won't be able to get away for a while. If it's urgent you may have to ring Dr Swain but I believe he's got a lot of surgery appointments right now.' She hesitated and added, 'We may even need him here, too.'

Kaycee thought rapidly. 'The patient's next dose of IV antibiotic is due in an hour. I'm not sure how urgent the IV fluids are either. Is. . .is it possible to ask him what he wants us to do?'

'I suppose I can interrupt and ask him. Just a moment, please.'

Kaycee heard the reluctance in her voice and wondered what could be happening there. She had heard that three women had been admitted to the labour ward over night. Normally Kaycee enjoyed her stints in Maternity but she had discovered a long time ago that although it was usually a very happy place to work in it could also be a very sad place.

Then she remembered that one of her old school friends was expecting her first baby in another six weeks and a pang of envy shot through her as she remembered the glow of happiness that had surrounded her friend the last time she saw her.

It was quite a while before she heard the phone picked up again at the other end.

'Kaycee, is that you?' Rowan's voice sounded weary and despondent.

A flood of feeling swept through Kaycee. She swallowed to clear her throat but her voice came out all wrong. 'I'm. . .I'm sorry to trouble you, Rowan, but Mrs Wilde's drip—'

'Yes, Joan told me,' he interrupted impatiently. 'I won't be able to leave here for quite a while. Mrs Wilde is the salmonella patient John admitted, isn't she?'

His voice was still doing all kinds of strange things to Kaycee's nervous system but she forced herself to crisply give him concise details about the patient.

'It sounds as though you can try her with more oral fluids. She should be rehydrated by now. If she doesn't start vomiting again she may not need the drip back in. However, she should still have the antibiotic given into the vein. Orally it might upset her stomach again.'

He paused and then added distractedly in a lowered voice, 'Oh, Kaycee, love, I. . .' He stopped abruptly and, after a moment, added more loudly, 'I have to go. I don't know how long I'll be here. Tell Sister if you're still worried about Mrs Wilde to give John Swain a ring.'

Kaycee replaced the phone slowly. What on earth could be happening? There had been such pain in his voice that she couldn't dredge up an ounce of regret that he had called her 'love'. In fact, a thrill of delight had swept through her at his low, intimate tone.

'I just hope no one else heard him,' she muttered out loud as she went off to give the RN the message

It did not take long for the grapevine to do its work. A fourteen-year-old had been brought into Emergency from the high school with severe abdominal pain. She was in labour and had not even realised that she was pregnant. Very soon after her admission the very premature baby had been still-born and it seemed for a while that the young mother would need a hysterectomy to stop the haemorrhaging. For the moment that had been averted.

The news cast a pall over the staff, who sympathised not only with the teenage mother and her shocked parents but with the staff in Maternity.

Kaycee couldn't stop thinking of Rowan for the rest of her shift. The patient she had rung him about had been given the IV antibiotic by one of the more senior sisters and was doing well on oral fluids, as Rowan had hoped.

Nevertheless, the extent of Kaycee's disappointment when Rowan did not come to the ward surprised her. Her ears had been strained every moment to hear him arrive and she sighed inwardly as she prepared to go home at the end of her shift without seeing him.

Then suddenly he was there, striding into the staff-room and murmuring a terse greeting to all and sundry but his dark eyes searching out and settling on Kaycee as she picked up her bag.

'You ready to leave?' His voice was abrupt and when she nodded wordlessly he added, 'Good, I'll get you to drive me home.'

Kaycee's face flamed at the small titter that came from one of the suddenly motionless staff.

Rowan's eyes swung in that direction. 'I've got a flat tyre on my car and I'm exhausted. You have a problem with that, Nurse?' he forcefully asked the tit-terer and then his gaze swung around the others and his voice dropped. 'What Nurse Wiseman and I do and any relationship we may or may not have is nobody's business but ours. I hope you all understand that.'

The challenge in very, very soft tones still held such a sting that no one moved.

Kaycee was galvanised into action. She strode forward.

'I'm sure they do, Dr Scott. Especially as you've been so kind as to point it out!'

She swept out of the room and headed down the corridor. He caught up with her as she reached the entrance to the hospital. Neither said a word as she stormed across the car park. He stood with his shoulders hunched as she unlocked her car.

'How *could* you embarrass us both like that? Now they'll all be absolutely convinced that the rumours are true. How on earth am I going to face them all next shift?' Kaycee glared at him as he swung his long legs into the passenger seat. 'For that piece of stupidity I ought to make you walk!'

He ignored her first slightly hysterical demand and merely said wearily, 'I wouldn't make it out of the car park.' He leaned back with a deep sigh and closed his eyes.

Suddenly she realised how pale and thoroughly exhausted he looked. She hesitated for a moment as she studied him and then all anger was swept away by anxiety. Hadn't he said once that he had been recovering from glandular fever when he was on holiday in Queensland? The hours he had been working since his arrival could very well bring on a relapse.

Without another word she started the car. He merely moved into a more comfortable position and was asleep before they had reached the centre of town. She hesitated for a moment and then made up her mind. His most pressing need was for undisturbed rest. Although he did not have the on-call pager clipped onto his belt at home he could be reached far too easily by phone, which John Swain was all too fond of doing.

Too bad. Let John Swain cope for a while without him.

That young man often did not pull his weight in the practice. She had heard rumours that Dr Gordon had received complaints about his lazy junior partner more than once in the past. Thank goodness today was Friday and Ian Taylor was expected to be back some time this evening.

Driving slowly out of town, she eventually turned off the bitumen onto a short gravel road. The car rolled gently to a stop under a magnificent old gum-tree. It was blissfully peaceful.

She feasted her eyes for a few moments on the

panorama in front of them. Grassy slopes rolled gently away from them to steeper hills thickly covered with thick bush and towering trees. Then she turned to study the man, who had still not stirred.

Very quickly he had earned the respect and admiration of the hospital staff and was now extremely popular. He came to see a patient when he said he would or let the staff know when he was delayed. This often saved a lot of time on the phone trying to find him. Both patients and staff were also more and more impressed by the fact that nothing seemed to miss his sharp eyes and intellect.

Her eyes softened as she remembered the young woman who had been so upset about needing a partial hysterectomy for severe endometriosis. He had been very patient, spending a lot of time with her and explaining in detail in language she could understand that the endometrium was the normal tissue lining of the uterine cavity but when it grew anywhere else it became a problem.

In her, it had invaded the uterus so badly that it would have to be removed to stop the severe pain and bleeding she had been periodically suffering. Fortunately, the visiting gynaecologist had not needed to touch her ovaries and so there was no need for her to worry about hormonal changes. It was bad enough that the sad young woman was facing a lifetime with the prospect of not being able to have children.

Somehow he had managed to squeeze in an appointment at the barber to have his unruly locks tamed. Her eyes traced the outline of his fair hair. When she had seen him yesterday for the first time with short hair she had turned quickly away, trying to conceal her disappointment and surprise at herself. He had looked much older, more mature and removed from her.

Her eyes drifted to his beautifully shaped mouth. Suddenly she wondered wistfully if she would ever feel them on her own again. Despite the change in his attitude towards her at work she was sure they could have spent some private time together if he had really wanted to.

She stiffened at the wayward thought and looked swiftly away. But the thought would not go. Despite his attitude to her at work he had been deliberately avoiding her. The more she thought about it the more she realised that it was true. She slipped a little further down in her seat and closed her eyes. Well, he couldn't get away from her now, no matter what. She had virtually kidnapped him!

A grin tilted her lips as she wondered what his reaction was going to be when he found out.

CHAPTER NINE

SOMETHING stroked gently across Kaycee's face. She stirred and sleepily raised a hand to brush it away and touched warm fingers that turned and grasped her own.

Kaycee jerked upright and looked full into Rowan's bemused face. They stared at each other for a moment without moving.

'Hi.'

As his lips moved a smile started in his eyes and she watched, fascinated, as it spread slowly across his face. It transformed him into the man who could take her breath away; the man she could never resist.

'Hello, yourself.' She had tried to make her voice nonchalant but it sounded husky instead. Her own lips softened into an answering smile.

His fingers tightened on her hand. 'Has anyone ever told you how incredibly beautiful you are?'

She opened her mouth and then closed it again. Speechless, she shook her head. His eyes drifted over her face and then settled on her lips. Her earlier wayward thoughts swept back. She was incapable of moving or even breathing.

With his eyes still on her mouth, he said softly, 'Where are we?'

He seemed to be fascinated as he watched her swallow and then her lips at last form the words, 'At. . .at the look-out.'

His head moved a little closer. Her eyes squeezed shut and she waited, expecting any moment to feel his lips possess hers. There was a pause and then she felt him move. The warmth of his hand was gone. Her eyes flew open to see that he had relaxed back onto the passenger's seat again and was gazing through the windshield. A muscle flexed in his jaw.

An unbelievable feeling of disappointment swept through her.

'And where is this look-out? And how far from the hospital are we?' His voice was mild but when he turned and looked at her she saw the censure in his eyes.

'Only about twenty minutes. And those forested little hills belong to the state forest,' she said quickly. 'You fell asleep and looked as though you could do with some peace.'

He was still watching her. Anger flickered across his face and he snorted. 'Peace? With you around?'

As soon as the sharp words had left him Rowan wished that he could recall them. He saw hurt whip through her and opened his mouth but he was too late. With quick movements she had opened her door and then slammed it so hard that he winced. He watched her stride away from him and his regret deepened. He was never quite sure if he wanted to grab her and kiss her senseless or put her across his knee and wallop her!

'You crazy woman,' he muttered. 'I didn't mean. . .'

He ran a hand through his hair in frustration. Just what had he meant? That when he was near this woman she disturbed him immensely? That she affected him as no woman ever had before, not even Sonja in the earliest crazy days of their relationship? That he had come within a hair's breadth of kissing her senseless a moment ago? She had been all temptation with her delicate fragrance and sweet innocence as she slept.

He groaned. He had tried so hard not to be alone

with her at the house. She was much too tempting. But, despite trying to keep his distance, Kaycee Wiseman was becoming far too important to him. And he wasn't at all sure that was a good idea! He wanted to live and work in a small town—hopefully, Coolong. But Kaycee seemed to hate small towns—Coolong in particular—and, according to her mother, she was set on moving to Sydney.

He had tried to get her mother to tell him why she had been so upset about the gossip. She had hesitated for a long time and then only confirmed what he had already worked out for himself.

'Gossip in the past has hurt this family badly.'

Then she had clammed up, stating firmly that the details were Kaycee's business and that she would tell him herself if she wanted to.

'Just don't you hurt my daughter, Rowan Scott,' Mrs Wiseman had said fiercely. 'She's been hurt enough.'

He had taken her mother's warning to heart and, besides, hadn't he vowed only last year not to get emotionally involved again with someone for a long time?

But in the past few weeks since then her mother had told him a lot about Kaycee, despite her reticence on that one issue. She had even talked on and on about her hope that one day her daughter would be able to do her nursing degree at university.

That had added to his determination not to get involved with Kaycee but he had still found himself at times rather concerned for her. It would mean Kaycee moving to a large city like Newcastle or even Sydney. She would love the novelty of it for a while but then. . .

What if she rushed into a relationship like he had had with Sonja? He had been so lonely that he had mistaken friendly feelings for love that he had hoped would be strong enough for the melding of both their careers and she had been friendly, outgoing. And after all these years Sonja was still being a pain in the neck, demanding to know when he was going to give up this nonsense about moving to the country.

He scowled. Despite all his resolves he really cared about what happened to Kaycee. Now he tried to tell himself that it was because she was just such a nice person. Over the weeks his admiration for Kaycee had increased more and more, not only for the strength she had been to her family but for her professional expertise and care for her patients.

Several times he had known she had stood up to less-experienced staff about her concerns over a patient, even though they had been her official superiors. And thank goodness she had over Ken Rodgers. Why on earth had Swain not had check-up X-rays done on his lungs before? Emphysema. She had been spot-on.

He climbed from the car and stretched, breathing deeply of the fresh country air. Kaycee was standing with her back to him. Her arms were wrapped around herself and she stared out across the paddocks, turning her head swiftly towards him and away again as he joined her. The wariness in her face suddenly lashed at him.

'I like Coolong. It's in a beautiful setting with the surrounding farmland and those mountains of forests.' Instead of looking at the view he studied her. Long eyelashes flickered as she blinked rapidly. Regretfully he noticed the way her mouth tightened. 'And it is very peaceful here but I should really be near a phone in case Swain needs me.'

She snorted. 'And I spoil the peace for you, anyway. I apologise. Let's go home, then.'

She started to turn away but he grabbed her arm. He said harshly, 'You've disturbed me far too much, Kaycee Wiseman, from the moment you crashed into me.'

'I can assure you the feeling is mutual,' she snapped back and then her expression changed as she realised what she had said.

For a moment they stared at each other and then, with a muffled exclamation, she jerked her arm free and spun away. Instead of heading for the car she made for a rough track through low scrub.

So he disturbed her, did he? Good. His spirits lifted. Then he scowled and started ambling thoughtfully after her.

He didn't want to be the one to bring more hurt to Kaycee. The moment those rumours about their supposed relationship had reached him he should have distanced himself from her completely, even stopped boarding at her house. Instead, he had convinced himself that treating her coldly at work would kill the rumours. That had apparently only fuelled them so he had tried to be natural with her. At least Bronwyn Brooks had stopped being all over him!

He grinned slightly. He had underestimated this country town. The only way to stop the rumours would have been to leave town altogether! But then Kaycee would have been the one to bear the brunt of speculation as to why he had left without her. He stopped smiling and sighed.

This very morning he had found himself taking her phone call in the middle of that whole tragic mess.

Inwardly he had been trying to understand how it

could be possible for a young teenager to be so ignorant in this day and age and he had just finished dealing with her distraught parents when Joan Allen had approached him with that most peculiar look on her face.

The sudden longing for contact with Kaycee had swamped him. He had needed her as he could not remember needing anyone ever before. There had been strange comfort in just hearing her voice. And after he had hung up, for a brief, mad moment he had wished fervently that the rumours were true—that he had the right to go to her, the right to wrap her in his arms and receive her comfort and her healing love.

But the memory of those feelings made him hesitate now. Not only did he not want to hurt this woman but he strongly suspected that she could have the ability to hurt him as Sonja never had.

When he at last caught up with Kaycee she was leaning against a guard rail and peering down. She ignored him as he drew level with her.

He controlled his voice with an effort. 'What's down there?' he asked softly. She pointed and at the same time he saw for himself and added, 'Ah, incredibly beautiful.'

Out of the corner of his eyes he saw Kaycee stiffen and fling a quick look at him. But he managed not to look at her; not to tell her again just how beautiful she was.

His hands clenched. There was nothing more he wanted than to pull her up against him. To kiss her senseless; to take all she would offer him. How much that would be, he dared not think about. But it would not be fair to her or to himself. He was an adult, for goodness' sake, not an immature boy any more—

grasping greedily for what he wanted, no matter whom he hurt.

Somehow he kept his gaze off Kaycee and on the beautiful evidence of spring and the promise of summer. The trees had thinned out considerably here. Across a gentle slope of waving grasses the huge jacaranda tree was glorious in its thick mantle of mauve blossoms. The purple blossoms of a bougainvillea climbing up through its branches spilled all down one side. As if that were not enough the tall silky oak tree beside it was still gleaming in the last rays of the western sun.

'Want a closer look?'

Her face was still averted but her voice was soft and he heard the slight wobble in it. His resistance withered. Without even thinking about it, he reached out and took her hand. She tensed but then relaxed and curled her fingers around his. They felt warm and strong. And right.

Still without speaking, she led him down a winding path. It had been a very warm spring day but now, as the last of the sunset's myriad colours began to disappear, a stillness surrounded them. They stopped simultaneously at the foot of the jacaranda tree. Standing on a carpet of mauve and purple blossoms, they looked up. There wasn't even the hint of a breeze. It seemed as though peace reached out and canopied them with the gentle blossoms.

Kaycee wondered if Rowan felt the wonder as she did. She dared to look swiftly at him and at the same moment he looked at her. At first it had hurt her deeply that he could not have peace near her. But then she had decided defiantly that she was glad. She wanted him to be as disturbed by her as she was by him.

She suddenly realised that he was watching her closely. There was a gentleness in his expression that she had not seen before. He smiled tenderly and then looked back up at the beauty before them.

Kaycee wanted to hold her breath; to hold onto the moment. As she stared at him all she could do was let her hand stay in his strong clasp.

It was some time before Rowan broke the silence. 'I noticed yesterday that one of the streets near the hospital was lined with jacarandas.'

As he spoke movement among clumps of tall grass some distance away caught their attention.

A large grey kangaroo had raised its head and stared straight at them. Kaycee caught her breath and unconsciously tightened her hold on Rowan's hand. Another smaller one nearby hopped a few paces and then bent its head to graze on the green grass again.

The large grey kangaroo continued to stare at them for a moment and then suddenly took fright. As he started bounding gracefully away several others they had not noticed lying under the scattered trees soon joined him and in a few moments they had all disappeared.

'It's been a long time since I saw a mob like that,' Rowan stirred and murmured rather wistfully a few moments later. 'And then they never seemed so grand—only pests competing with sheep for our pastures.'

Kaycee turned and looked at him. 'Whereabouts did you grow up?'

He glanced at her briefly and then turned back to where the kangaroos had disappeared. 'Central west New South Wales. On a wheat and sheep station between Dubbo and Gilgandra. Drought, low prices and high interest rates, as well as an overpopulation of kangaroos, eventually forced my dad to sell up when I was only fourteen.'

He shrugged and added sadly, 'An old story but all too familiar these days. Farm had been in the family for generations.'

He turned to her and reached out and grabbed her other hand, holding it firmly. Kaycee found her fingers had a will of their own and curled tightly around the much larger hands.

They studied each other for a long moment. His expression had changed but Kaycee could not read anything of his thoughts.

A little desperately she asked, 'Did you always want to be a doctor?'

Rowan gave a low laugh. 'Nope, I always took it for granted I'd grow up and work with my dad on the farm and then take over from him one day like he had with his father. When he lost the farm we settled in Dubbo. It wasn't until my high school results started looking very promising that I gave any serious thought to what else I could do with my life except farming.

'Or rather, my sister Elle started giving it serious thought after. . .' He paused for a moment, and then added softly, 'After my parents were killed, Elle finished bringing me up.'

Kaycee gave a murmur of distress and his eyes returned swiftly to her face. 'Car accident,' he said tersely, answering the unspoken question in her eyes. 'On a long, straight stretch of country road. Police said high speed and a tyre blowout. I was fifteen and Elle seventeen.'

There was such remembered pain in his face that instinctively Kaycee put her arms around him. His body was taut for a moment and then he relaxed against her. But he only gave her a quick hug and pushed her gently away.

Her arms seemed to have a mind of their own, she thought despairingly as embarrassment flooded her and she jerkily moved away.

Rowan caught her hands again and restrained her gently. 'It was a long time ago. Sometimes I feel more sad that there are so many things now I can't remember about them.'

After a moment she ventured, 'And Elle?'

He gave a snort. 'She brought me up with a rod of iron, you might say. At least, until I left for med school, it felt like that. Now I know it was partly her way of handling her own grief and the responsibility of a teenager. You remind me of her sometimes, Kaycee,' he added abruptly.

She kept her gaze steady with an effort. 'Is that a good thing or a bad thing?'

To her dismay, he dropped her hands and turned away. 'I'm not sure,' he muttered, again staring away to where the kangaroos had disappeared.

And so, Kaycee thought wearily, if he feels anything for me it's probably more like a brother than anything or because he feels sorry for Drew!

At last she said huskily, 'Your sister did a good job. You've done very well, Rowan. She must be very proud of you.'

He snorted. 'You think so?'

'At least you had the chance to go to uni—to do what you wanted to.'

He must have heard the trace of envy in her voice and turned round sharply. 'It would seem so, wouldn't it? But I've known for a long time how true that old over-used saying is about putting a country boy into the city but not being able to take the country out of the boy.

'I've grown to hate the noise, the mad rush of people and traffic in Sydney! I never want to live in a big city again. Despite the hordes of people rushing about their business I've met more lonely people there than farmers living miles from their nearest neighbour.'

He meant it. There was no mistaking the firm voice and determined expression on his face. He really hated the city. She stared at him sadly.

'But you do enjoy being a doctor?'

He studied her thoughtfully for a long moment. 'Yes, I do. Very much, in fact. But I was beginning to not like myself very much in Sydney. Patients came and went and suddenly I realised that's all I was thinking they were. Patients who were there to further my career. Not sick and hurting people who needed my training and expertise so as many as possible could be made well and whole physically *and* emotionally.'

'But that would not be only your fault, Rowan,' Kaycee said swiftly.

He stared at her silently.

'It's the fault of the whole system. It happens in Coolong, too. Too many hurting people, not enough staff and not enough hours in the day to do all we would like to for patients—besides what time and money dictate are really, after all, only the bare essentials.'

She smiled a little crookedly at him and then turned away. 'I suppose you've been too long away from a phone with only Dr Swain around. We'd better go,' she added abruptly.

'Kaycee?'

She paused and looked at him. Rowan's eyes were staring at her with a strange intensity. A solitary mauve bell drifted silently and slowly down between them.

He put out a hand. For the life of her she couldn't stop her own reaching out. It curled around his again. He held it between both of his and stared down at them for a long moment.

Then he sighed and looked up at her. 'Your mother told me that the death of your father prevented you from going to Sydney as you had planned to get your nurse's degree.'

Kaycee forced herself to look steadily back at him. 'You and Mum been having some cosy gossip sessions about me, have you?'

The strange expression on his face disappeared. He gave a low chuckle. 'According to your mother, you are the most beautiful, wonderful, clever daughter a woman could ever have.'

'I don't believe you,' Kaycee said flatly. She tried to tug her hand free but his grip tightened.

His face sobered. 'Why would you say that, Kaycee?'

'Because. . .because. . .' Words failed her and again she tugged on her hands and he let them go.

She turned her back on him and it was her turn to stare blindly across the paddocks. 'Evidently you didn't hear as much that night as I thought. I believed rumours were true about her having an affair and that it indirectly contributed to Dad's death.'

After a moment she added in a choked voice, 'Although that's only part of it. Mainly it's because any self-confidence she may have had left after those awful years I helped take away from her by my unforgiving and judgemental attitude.'

He was silent for a long moment. 'Your mother told me she doesn't think she would have survived that first couple of years without you.'

She swung around and searched his face wordlessly.

'It's true, sweetheart. She said she thinks she must have been very close to a mental and physical breakdown.'

Kaycee shook her head. 'Then her generosity makes my behaviour even worse. I've been thinking that she must have sensed my condemnation of her and that that was extra pressure on her. Deep down I've even blamed her because I was stuck in this. . .this hole of a town.'

She sighed and continued unsteadily, 'These last few weeks I've had to come to grips with the fact that the only person I have to blame is myself. I could have left years ago. Jan had a good job in Newcastle for a year before she got married. She offered some of her salary but I refused. Mum and Andrew would have coped.'

'Not until you'd paid the last of the mortgage on the house off with your salary.'

She scowled at him. 'Is there anything she hasn't told you?'

His eyes lit up again with the familiar gleam of fun and amusement that she had seen often lately at the hospital. 'Oh, yes, certainly. She hasn't told me what you would say if I told you that, right at this moment, there's nothing I'd like to do more than kiss you senseless.'

'Well, you don't have to ask my mother's permission for that!'

As soon as the sharp words had left her mouth Kaycee gasped and turned to flee. She didn't know what it was about this man that made words spill out of her in a way she had never dreamt of!

Rowan moved fast. He caught her before she had taken more than two steps. 'Oh, no, you don't! Not after that provocative statement.'

There was a slight tussle and then Kaycee subsided and let his strong arms pull her close up against him. Brown eyes stared into blue for a moment. All amusement fled and that strange, intent look turned Rowan's eyes to a deep purple. Then they blurred and were hidden as his lips descended.

Her breath left her in a little sigh and her own hands went around him to hold him even closer. This time strong lips did touch hers, gently at first. Her own quivered and suddenly he deepened the kiss.

Then she kissed him back.

Hard.

It seemed like for ever before he released her enough so that she could lean back far enough in his arms to stare dreamily up at him. They were both breathless.

She thought he looked stunned. So, who had kissed who senseless? she wondered with considerable satisfaction.

One of her trembling, wondering fingers traced one thick eyebrow. Slowly it moved up to lightly touch the hair that was now too short to flop over onto his forehead in a curl.

'I shouldn't have done that,' he muttered suddenly.

Her hand stilled. Sadness welled up in her as she remembered what he had said about living in a city—about his sister. A tremor passed through Rowan's lithe body. His grip tightened and his soft groan was like a prayer.

Kaycee tensed.

'I'm afraid we are very close to doing exactly what the old gossips in this town have already had us doing.'

His soft words were like a douche of cold water. Kaycee's hand fell empty to her sides.

His arms tightened. He squeezed his eyes shut for a moment. Then he opened them and studied her silently.

After a long moment he muttered huskily, 'Bad move, Scott!'

Kaycee wrenched away from his warmth. She stared back at eyes that had rapidly filled with remorse and self-condemnation. Then abruptly she turned away.

An affair. Was that all he wanted?

For herself she knew that it wasn't even an option. There was no way that she would ever be able to make love to someone unless there was the type of love that needed a commitment on both sides. And, for her, commitment without marriage had always seemed a very weak kind indeed.

That had been a decision that she had made all those years ago when she had thought her mother had. . .had. . . But she'd been wrong, hadn't she? Her mother had never had an affair, after all.

Rowan watched her turn and flee from him back to the car. His body still ached to be held in her compelling arms. The pounding of his heart was taking a long, long time to slow down. His breathing was still rapid.

At last he moved forward slowly, trying to come to grips with the passion that she had aroused in him.

No, it wasn't merely passion.

That had been with Sonja. This was different, very different. Perhaps his ex-fiancée had been right after all when she had accused him of never really loving her. Certainly, never before had he cared so much about other people's attitude to a woman he was attracted to;

never cared so much that she not be hurt by anyone or anything, especially by himself.

Kaycee had almost reached the car when she stopped. She waited for him to get closer and then she said bluntly, without looking at him, 'I think it would be best if you found somewhere else to stay as soon as possible.'

Astonishment flashed through him. And then he was surprised at the extent of the dismay that followed. He remained silent until she flicked a glance at him. His heart contracted. Her mouth was set but her eyes were dark pools of confusion and pain.

He looked back at her steadily. 'Has your mother found a buyer for the house already?'

She shook her head abruptly. 'No one's even looked at it yet. It's the gossip I'm worried about.'

Anger stirred in Rowan but, before he could say what he thought of that, she snapped, 'You thought I'd deliberately fostered those rumours, didn't you?'

His eyebrows went up in genuine astonishment and he flashed back, 'Why on earth would I think that when you so obviously didn't want to have anything to do with me?'

It was her turn to look surprised. 'But I didn't. . .I mean. . .' She gulped and added, with a frown, 'Then why on earth were you so unfriendly and even nasty to me at the beginning?'

'Was I really that bad, Kaycee?'

Kaycee couldn't take her eyes from his. They had darkened as they had just before he had kissed her. His voice was a little wistful but she refused to soften.

'Yes, you were,' she said firmly. 'One of the worst times was when you bawled me out for getting Brett Porter out of bed and into a chair to make his bed before you had given permission——when you already had.'

Rowan scowled. 'You're mistaken. I had given specific instructions he was to remain on bedrest until I had seen him that day. I wanted to be certain there was no paralysis and that his kidney function was still improving. If I remember correctly I arrived to find him already on his feet being assisted to a chair by you.'

'But Bronwyn Brooks had told me it was all right to—— Oh!'

They stared at each other. Kaycee knew now why Sister Brooks had been so sympathetic and nice to her for the rest of that day. She had achieved her purpose of putting Kaycee in a bad light with the man she had her own eye on.

A flare of emotion shot through her. Kaycee was horribly afraid that it was jealousy!

She flinched and moved abruptly, hoping that he had not been able to read her expression. 'But why do that when you were already showing how much you disliked me?'

'Perhaps I'm a bad actor after all,' he murmured gently.

She stared at him, uncertain of what he meant, and then swung away. 'Anyway, you still didn't have to be so sarcastic and horrible about it. And there were plenty of other times, too.'

'I thought it might stop those stupid rumours.'

'Well, it didn't! Everyone thought it was only camouflage. According to Jill, it only fuelled the idea that we had something to hide!'

Refusing to look at him in case he could see how really hurt she had been by some of the things he had said to her, Kaycee reached out to open the car door.

Correction, she thought. It had not been so much

what he had said as how he had said it. What had hurt even more were the times that he had completely ignored her.

'But you do have to admit I've been much nicer to you lately.' There was quiet humour in his voice.

Her hand closed convulsively on the doorhandle. Suddenly she knew why he'd had the ability to hurt her so much. Why she had just felt that flare of jealousy.

'I wasn't only trying to stop the rumours, Kaycee.'

Kaycee was still trying to deal with her new knowledge about her feelings. It took a moment for his soft words to penetrate. She held her breath.

'Well, at least by the time Brett was out of High Dependency my motive had changed somewhat.'

There was a strained, husky note in his voice that had her turning around slowly. She stared at him for a moment, hardly daring to believe the soft expression that had crept into his face.

'By then I was fighting like crazy the wish that there was a chance the darned rumours would come true. And that made me mad.' His voice had deepened to a husky whisper. As he looked deeply into her eyes, he cleared his throat. 'Especially when I had momentarily thought that first night I heard them that you must have started them yourself.'

She had known it. That was why he had been so angry.

Kaycee found her voice at last. 'That very first night!' She remembered how she had been so exhausted but had not wanted to go to bed until she had seen him again. 'So you lied to me a moment ago. Thanks for having such a high opinion of me!'

'I just told you it was only for the briefest moment. There's an unmistakable integrity about you. In fact, I felt dreadfully guilty for entertaining the idea for even a moment,' he added rapidly.

A look of regret came into his eyes. His voice changed subtly. 'It had happened to me once before. Rumours and dangerous gossip happens in cities as well as small towns, Kaycee. A woman deliberately started some rumours. It caused me a lot of embarrassment with my strait-laced, old-fashioned boss who still believed that a doctor's personal life should be above reproach.'

'A woman actually started rumours that you. . .that you. . .' Kaycee found it hard to picture. 'But what on earth did she hope to achieve?'

A wry grin tilted his lips. 'A case of a woman scorned?'

'Oh.'

'But I realised that you could have no such motive.'

'You did?'

Kaycee hardly knew what she was saying. There was something decidedly mesmerising about staring into those fascinating, sparkling blue eyes. She couldn't tell just what he was really thinking but hope quivered through her as she listened to the low, husky voice that had dropped almost to a whisper again.

'I could never scorn you, Kaycee, sweetheart.'

They stared at each other. There still wasn't the hint of a breeze and it was as though the very air had forgotten to breathe.

'This is ridiculous,' Kaycee murmured a little desperately at long last. 'We hardly know each other.'

She didn't think his eyes could have darkened even further but they did.

'How long does it take to know, I wonder?' His

finger gently traced her cheek. 'But—know each other for what, Kaycee?'

'For. . .for friendship, let alone. . .let alone. . .' Her voice choked and faded helplessly away.

'Let alone being lovers?'

His soft murmur reached her from only a breath away. Then even that distance was gone as his lips settled onto hers. For a moment she was still and then his lips moved and their warmth and fullness seemed strangely very familiar. . .very right. . .

Eons later there was the blare of a horn as a small truck went hurtling past the look-out, leaving a thick cloud of dust that settled over them and got into their eyes and caused them to gasp and splutter.

When they had recovered, Rowan was grinning. With a flourish he held open her car door for her. 'Give me a nice peaceful park in Sydney any day! Truckies seem to be out to get us!'

Automatically she climbed in and tried to gather her scattered wits as he walked around the car and settled in his own seat. She didn't reach for the ignition key but just sat staring blindly through the windscreen.

'Kaycee, would you like me to drive?'

She started, darted a look at him and shook her head. How was she to say what had to be said to him? How did she convince herself that it had to be said? Especially after her response to that last mind-destroying embrace.

'I'm afraid I really shouldn't be away from a phone any longer, Kaycee. Thank goodness there'll be three of us docs again after tonight.'

She was poised on the brink of a cliff and all he could think about was his work!

But his almost expressionless voice helped her.

Somewhere she dredged up the self-control and values of a lifetime to say quietly, 'I don't want an affair with you, Rowan.'

She wasn't brave enough to look at him but just turned the key in the ignition. As the motor roared to life she heard him murmur his response. She glanced quickly at him, not sure if her ears had heard him correctly. He was smiling slightly, which confused her even more.

She thought he had murmured, 'Good!'

He never said another word all the way home.

She wasn't quite game enough to ask him to repeat what he had said. Or to quiz him further.

Because, after the way he had looked at her. . .kissed her. . .touched her. . .what on earth was she supposed to make of that one confusing word?

CHAPTER TEN

FOR the next few days Kaycee was very wary around Rowan. She relaxed gradually as not once did he attempt to see her on her own. At least away from work. There it was a different matter.

He gently and affectionately teased her, always in front of someone, literally beaming at her when he succeeded in making her laugh. She had begun to suspect that he even went out of his way to make sure that he visited her patients when she was on duty. The attitude of a couple of the other nurses seemed to confirm that. It was almost as if he was trying to convince everyone just how highly he thought of her as a person and a nurse.

To say that Dr Rowan Scott was more open in his friendliness to her in front of the staff would be an understatement, she had thought grimly several times. He was positively lover-like.

Away from the knowing eyes at work—some expressing strong disapproval—he was anything but lover-like. He even seemed to be avoiding her. Where before he had seemed happy enough to share meals and the occasional moments alone together when their shifts allowed now she found that he was always out and about and they never spent time in each other's presence unless her mother was there.

Even on his days off he had made trips away overnight, not giving her a clue where he had gone. Careful

questioning of her mother revealed that he had not
breathed a word to her either.

When they did meet unexpectedly away from the
hospital, he spoke to her quietly but briefly. He never
made any attempt to touch her and only now did she
realise how often before he had run that finger down
her cheek; pushed a strand of wayward hair behind her
ear; held her hand. Instead, the tension built up between
them more and more.

Sometimes, as she stared mournfully at her ceiling
when unable to sleep, she thought that they could have
been mere acquaintances; not a man and a woman who
had shared beautiful, intimate moments; not a man and
woman who had known sheer ecstasy when they kissed
and clung.

A few times at home, at mealtimes or watching television, she had thought that he was staring at her. But
always he had either looked away quickly or—what
was more likely, she had decided grimly—she had only
been indulging in wishful thinking.

It was a fortnight after she had kidnapped him that
Rowan and Kaycee shared a rare evening meal together
with Mrs Wiseman. Kaycee had been determinedly
chatty, trying desperately to dispel the tension between
her and the polite, distant man. For the two previous
days he had become more and more withdrawn, even
at work, and Kaycee's misery had increased.

'I'm moving out, Mrs Wiseman,' he suddenly said
abruptly, rudely cutting right across Kaycee, who was
in the middle of telling them something from one of
Andrew's letters.

Moving out. Kaycee stared blankly at him, her
despair complete.

There and then she decided that if loving someone,

like she increasingly loved this infuriating Dr Rowan Scott, made a woman as miserable and bewildered as she felt right now then she was very glad that she had never suffered this affliction before!

He had taken her stupid words seriously and found somewhere else to live. One part of her felt relief. At least she would not have to brace herself every time she came face to face with him unexpectedly at home. But it was that other deep part of her that was protesting loudly.

'Mr Rodgers's daughter recently moved out of the flat at the back of his place and he's letting me take it,' she realised Rowan was saying calmly.

'How fortunate, Rowan,' Mrs Wiseman said brightly, 'both for you and Ken Rodgers. As you can move straight in he doesn't lose any rent after his daughter moves out. And he still has someone nearby if his health gets bad again.'

'It's fully furnished, too.' Rowan smiled at her gently. 'I only have to get my own linen and crockery up from Sydney.'

'But you haven't got much longer before your time filling in for Dr Gordon is finished, have you?' burst out Kaycee. 'Is it worth all the trouble of moving when you'll be gone soon anyway? Unless. . . Mum! You haven't sold the house, have you?'

Rowan turned to Kaycee and something flared in his eyes that she could not interpret.

Mrs Wiseman bit her lip and glanced quickly at Rowan. 'Well, as a matter of fact, someone has been talking to me about the possibility of buying. But nothing's by any means definite,' she added hurriedly. She looked wistfully across the scattered remains of their dinner at her daughter and asked gently, 'Do you still mind very much if the house is sold, Kaycee?'

Kaycee swept a hand across the side of her head, tucking away a few strands of hair. She looked around the beautiful room and then her eyes were drawn back to the man sitting near her. Suddenly she wondered how she could live here, or anywhere for that matter, without him coming. . .going. . .

Rowan was staring at her very intently. He held her gaze for a moment and then looked down at his now-empty dessert bowl. Anguish swept through her.

'This has been the only home I've ever known,' she murmured huskily at last. Then she forced a smile for her mother. 'But, no, I don't really mind, I guess.' She stood up and added impulsively, 'In fact, Mum, I've decided to try and get work in Sydney.'

'Work?' Mrs Wiseman sounded disappointed. 'But what about trying to get into uni to do your nursing degree?'

Kaycee could feel Rowan's eyes on her but deliberately avoided them. 'Oh, Mum, dear,' she said gently, 'I gave up that idea years ago. Besides, I've decided that I'm only interested in hands-on nursing and being an EN gives me plenty of that! What I really want to try is to develop my art work. There are plenty of colleges and courses where I can do that in Sydney. Now,' she added abruptly, 'I need an early night so I'll start on the dishes.'

Still not looking toward Rowan, she started collecting the dirty plates. This time she would be the one to leave the room first.

Rowan said quietly, 'I haven't got only a few weeks left in Coolong, Kaycee.'

The plates she had picked up clattered slightly in her

hands. She put them down carefully and her eyes flew to look at him at last. He was still studying her intently.

'But wasn't Dr Gordon going to be away only three months? He should be back soon.'

'Yes,' responded Rowan a little curtly, 'and you misunderstand. I've agreed to stay longer—until at least the end of December. John Swain is leaving. Besides, we all think that the practice needs an extra doctor. I must say, I wholeheartedly agree,' he added fervently.

Once the three doctors had been all back at work the place had quietened down but they had still been kept busy. There had been no further emergencies except the usual minor injuries. Brett Porter had remained in hospital for a couple of weeks longer than his brother but was now again terrorising the neighbourhood, according to Mrs Wiseman who had kept contact with the family.

'Are. . .are you going to join the practice permanently?' The long-held-in question burst out of Kaycee and was immediately regretted.

Rowan frowned. He opened his mouth but Mrs Wiseman said reprovingly, 'That's none of our business, Kaycee. Rowan shouldn't discuss something like that until things are settled. You know how rumours spread!'

'Yes,' Rowan agreed harshly. He pushed back his chair abruptly and stood up. 'We all know about rumours in this town. But I know neither of you will repeat this. Yes, I have been offered a partnership but I haven't made a decision yet.'

He stared across at Kaycee with that same intent look as before. For a moment she thought he was going to say something else but his glance flickered to her mother, his jaw clenched and he turned and stalked out of the room.

Kaycee sadly watched him leave the room. But he would accept it, she knew. She had heard him say several times how much he liked the town and district. And he especially loved the mountains with their many forest trails and camping spots. It was time she, too, made some decisions about where she was going to live.

Rowan still wanted the country. Her desire to have a taste of city life had only been strengthened these last weeks. Even if. . .

She shook off the thought immediately. No, he had decided that they were too different; wanted too different a lifestyle. She would just have to accept the fact that there could be no future for them together.

It didn't help to have her mother voice her own thoughts out loud. 'Well, I think he'll be staying in Coolong a long time. He's already very highly spoken of.' Mrs Wiseman stood up and then paused. 'Kaycee, have you spoken to Andrew lately?'

With an effort Kaycee focused on her. 'Drew? No,' she said slowly. 'Come to think of it, I've only spoken to him once since he was home. He's never been in other times I've tried. Sounded very bubbly and happy when I did speak to him.'

Mrs Wiseman frowned.

'Why, Mum? Nothing's wrong, is there?'

'I'm not sure,' her mother responded slowly. 'His last letter seemed OK, too. But there's been something different about him, even when he was home for his birthday. He's been very moody. He snapped my head off the other night when I rang him.' She shrugged.

'Oh, well, apparently he finishes exams and assignments this coming week and he did say how busy he was with study and working a few hours each week at that restaurant. Guess he'll just need a good long rest over the holidays.'

Which he isn't going to get if he works full time at that restaurant as he hoped, worried Kaycee silently. I'll go down and see him next week, she decided suddenly. His exams will be over by then and it'll be good to get away from here too.

A few days later Rowan moved out.

Being inland, Coolong usually escaped the humidity of the coastal regions but that late spring day was unusually hot and steamy. The old-timers in the district predicted thunderstorms and, by the afternoon, Bronwyn Brooks voiced all their thoughts when she said fervently that she hoped they were right.

'Anything to cool down the place,' she added irritably. 'When will the powers that be decide we do need air-conditioning?' Then she snarled at Kaycee, 'Better offer all your patients extra fluids, Nurse.'

Kaycee nodded briefly, not bothering to explain that she had been doing that all day. She had been calmly going about her work, trying not to let the heat bother her or her patients too much or thoughts of Rowan intrude.

He had said something a couple of days ago about going to Sydney today to bring back a load of his things but whether he had or not she did not know.

That morning Bob was driving her mother to Canberra to be with Jan until her baby was born—hopefully during the coming week. And, although she had heard Rowan thumping around in his room very early, he had not come out to say goodbye before she had left for work. So Kaycee knew that the house would be empty when she arrived home and for once she was in no hurry to finish her shift.

When she did eventually walk listlessly past the front reception area on her way off duty a flustered-looking receptionist called out to her.

'Nurse Wiseman, could you help us, please?'

Kaycee reluctantly turned towards her. A short, dainty-looking blonde, standing in front of the desk on very high heels, swung around and surveyed her with a look of disdain.

As she drew near the blonde said haughtily, 'This woman seems to think you can tell me where Dr Scott is.' She looked Kaycee up and down doubtfully.

'I told you, Dr Power, that he boards at Nurse Wiseman's home.' This usually calm and competent receptionist sounded rattled. 'That is the only address we have.'

The stranger's eyes narrowed. 'But the address he told me to go to was only at the back of an old house. It was dreadfully small,' she said accusingly. 'And there was no one about when I did eventually find it,' she added angrily, as though that had been a personal affront. 'He assured me he would be there.'

Kaycee swallowed, striving as hard as she could not to let either woman see how this upset her. She forced a polite smile at the receptionist. 'Dr Scott moved into the flat only today. I'm sure he'll give you the new address and phone number as soon as he can.' Turning to the woman, she said quietly, 'I understand Dr Scott intended going to Sydney today.'

'But he couldn't have! I've just come from there,' Dr Power said furiously. 'I'm Sonja Power, his fiancée. Now what am I supposed to do with his things?'

The face in front of Kaycee tilted and dimmed. Her mouth went dry.

So that was why Rowan had backed off from their relationship. All the time this woman had been waiting for him.

Kaycee made a tremendous effort and at last managed to say faintly, 'His things?'

'His belongings that were still at my flat. Why on earth he ever was crazy enough to come to work in this one-horse place. . .' She stopped abruptly, her eyes widening at Kaycee. 'Your name wouldn't be Kaycee by any chance?'

Speechless, Kaycee nodded. Fortunately the fascinated receptionist had been forced to answer the phone and there was no witness to the strange expression that filled Dr Power's face.

She stared at Kaycee, examining her closely. 'He *must* be mad!'

For a moment Kaycee thought that she must have misheard the muttered words. Then she felt a crimson tide flood her face.

As much as she knew it would hurt, she had been wondering if she should offer this woman some hospitality but instead she snapped, 'I can assure you that Dr Scott is perfectly sane.'

At least I hope he is if this is the type of woman that appeals to him, she almost added.

Gathering all her courage, she straightened to her full height. For once she was glad of the advantage it gave her. She looked down her nose and said abruptly, 'Now, if you can't wait for him the only thing I can suggest is that you give me whatever things you have for him. I'll make sure he gets them. My car's this way.'

She turned and started for the door without looking

back, not particularly caring if the woman took her up on her offer or not. She was halfway down the front steps before there was a clatter of heels and Dr Power followed her.

'But couldn't I just go home with you and wait until he turns up?' a slightly breathless voice said plaintively when Kaycee paused beside her car.

'I'm afraid that's not possible,' Kaycee said curtly, not giving an inch. 'There's a motel on the outskirts of town if you need accommodation. You might have to book in as soon as you can. There happens to be a cattle sale there in a couple of days.'

And I hope they bawl all night and keep you awake, too, she thought viciously as she helped carry boxes from a streamlined, late-model sedan to her own battered little car.

When they had finished Kaycee felt hotter and grubbier than ever. She wished the beautiful, petite woman a curt farewell, determined to ignore the look of barely concealed amusement that had been on the woman's face the whole time in the car park.

On the way home Kaycee took a detour and drove past Ken Rodgers's place. There was no sign of the red sports car so, without stopping, she headed for home. Just as well, she thought furiously. I'd probably have strangled him!

There was a strange vehicle parked there. It was one of the large four-wheel-drive-type wagons that were often used on the rough trails through the state forests by enthusiastic campers and bush walkers.

To her dismay the front door of the house was wide open. Her anger and pain was quickly replaced by apprehension. Crime wasn't altogether unknown in

Coolong—even burglaries. She hesitated only briefly before very quietly tiptoeing inside.

'Kaycee?'

She relaxed with a little gasp of fright as Rowan came down the hallway. And then she hurried forward at his grave expression.

'What's wrong? I thought you'd still be in Sydney. . .'

Her voice died away as his fingers went to his lips to hush her. Then he shrugged as another, drowsy voice called out.

'It's me, Sis. I'm home.'

Kaycee started forward but Rowan grasped her arm and whispered fiercely, 'He's going to be OK but don't let him see how shocked you are. I'll explain later.'

She stared at him blankly and then pushed past him, fear drenching her as she rushed into the lounge room. Despite Rowan's warning there would have been no way that she could have hidden her horrified expression immediately from her brother if he had not been lying back in a chair with his eyes closed.

He was so dreadfully thin and pale that he could have just arrived from one of those overseas countries that were being sent food and aid for their starving multitudes.

'Well, I've just sorted out your room for you, Drew,' Rowan said cheerfully from behind Kaycee. 'Sorry, Kaycee, but Drew said he preferred his own old bed over the one in the room I'd just moved out of. Come on, mate, you might as well go and sleep on your bed now instead of that lounge chair.'

Kaycee was too upset to do more than stare at her brother as he slowly uncurled himself and stood up. Only Rowan's hand on her arm prevented her from racing to help him as he walked unsteadily towards them.

'Do you know that this bloke slept all the way home in the car from Newcastle?' Rowan's voice held only affectionate amusement but his grip on her arm tightened as Andrew stumbled past them.

'Sorry, Sis,' Andrew muttered in a dazed voice. 'Been overdoing it a bit. Finished last exam yesterday. Need sleep.'

Kaycee found her voice. She glared furiously at Rowan and shrugged him off to follow the swaying figure down the hall. As steadily as she could she said, 'What about something to eat first?'

The tall figure stumbled and grabbed the open bedroom door.

'Not hungry.' Andrew's voice was irritable. 'Doc made me eat so don't you start, Kaycee!'

She turned and looked at Rowan. He shook his head warningly at her and she swung back, just in time to have the bedroom door slammed in her face.

For a moment she hesitated and then she whirled around. Before she had done more than open her mouth Rowan had grabbed her and started bundling her back the way they had come.

'Easy, Kaycee, let him be.'

'But what's wrong with him? Is he sick? He. . .he looks absolutely dreadful!'

Rowan didn't answer until he had pushed her onto a chair in the kitchen. She stared up at him helplessly and noticed for the first time the strain on his face.

'Unfortunately your brother has been stupid enough to fall into one of the many traps that university students these days often do.'

Fearfully she asked, 'What. . .what do you mean?'

Then her eyes widened in horror. 'Not. . .not drugs?' she whispered.

Rowan nodded briefly. 'Ever nursed anyone on amphetamines, Kaycee?'

For a moment Kaycee couldn't speak. Then she faltered, 'No. . .I don't think. . . Oh, one of my friends told me one of her kids has to take it for hyperactivity but what has that go to do. . .? No. . .!'

Her voice faded away and tears welled in her eyes. She had remembered the more commonly known term for the stimulant when obtained illegally.

Until now Rowan had managed to suppress the rage that had been flooding him since he had first seen Andrew Wiseman. He had known how much this would devastate his sister. Now he couldn't bear to see her distress.

'Speed, it's called,' he said furiously. 'And I'm one of many doctors who believe its only legitimate use is for narcolepsy or hyperactive kids. Instead of admitting he couldn't cope the silly idiot let his flat-mates talk him into using the filthy stuff earlier in the year to keep awake to finish assignments.

'They became worried about him this last couple of weeks when he took it nearly all the time but were too irresponsible to contact anyone. Probably thought they'd all be in trouble with the police.'

A sob tore through the woman staring at him with anguish in her face. With a muffled groan he hauled her into his arms.

'Oh, Kaycee, sweetheart, if only I'd gone to see him weeks ago. I suspected there was something not quite right the day I first met him.'

A tremor passed through the girl. 'Mum noticed

something too, but I was too busy organising everybody to notice!'

Kaycee pulled back and reluctantly he let her go.

Dazed, tear-drenched eyes stared up at him. 'You said something about going to Sydney today,' she said in an unsteady voice. 'Did you call in on the way, or. . .?'

'Bob Gould rang me from Newcastle. Fortunately I was here still packing. They left early so they could call in to see Andrew on their way through. He was sleeping very heavily and was extremely irritable when they disturbed him. He refused to talk to them so Bob rounded up one of his so-called friends, and, from what I can understand, threatened him with the police but literally shook the truth out of him.'

The man she had thought insignificant—even a bit wimpish—because he was so quiet? Kaycee shook her head to clear it. Bob Gould shaking the truth out of someone?

'Apparently Andrew's been popping pills increasingly since his party and then even more these last weeks so he could get through the exams. They think he took the last one yesterday morning before his last test. Your mother wanted to haul him off to the hospital but Bob persuaded her to ring me first. They were both ready to put off their trip to your sister. I convinced them that we could cope.'

Kaycee had been staring at him the whole time he had rattled out the bare bones of the story. He didn't bother to tell her that he had cancelled his own trip to Sydney the day before for other reasons entirely or how hard it had been to convince her mother that he would look after both of her offspring back in Coolong.

'But. . .but why is he so dreadfully thin?' Kaycee wailed.

'Because one of the many unpleasant side-effects of amphetamines is appetite suppression. He simply hasn't been eating much at all.'

Rowan hesitated and then, as her anxious, tear-filled eyes implored him, he said crisply, 'The risk of him having become psychologically dependent on them is hopefully not too great. Apparently he's only taken them very spasmodically until recently. He'd got behind on assignments and took them to stay awake until he'd finished them. If we can believe what we've been told that was much earlier in the year and then only again a couple of days before the party. Until now. He's only been on them regularly this last couple of weeks. Hopefully he's sensible enough to have learnt a good lesson.'

'And. . .and what about physical withdrawal symptoms?'

'Well, most authorities believe physical dependence is still open to question and mainly any dependence appears to be psychological,' he assured her hurriedly. 'However, as you can see, his body is demanding that it be allowed to catch up on sleep. For a few days don't be surprised if he sleeps anything up to twenty hours a day.'

He hesitated but decide that she was too good a nurse not to realise there would be more. 'We're all going to need a great deal of patience, I'm afraid, sweetheart,' he added very gently. 'Profound apathy and depression, lethargy and overeating, as well as fatigue and pro-longed sleep, characterise immediate withdrawal. It's going to depend on just how long and how many he's been taking. It could last several days.'

He watched her shoulders slump even more. Then she straightened, reached out and grabbed a tissue and wiped her face in such a businesslike way that his heart melted.

What was it about this woman that affected him like this? He had been using every bit of will-power he could muster since he had lost his self-control at the look-out. He didn't want to push her into something before she was ready or himself either, for that matter.

The gallant, resolute smile that she suddenly gave him broke down his last resistance. 'Well, then, I'd better ring the hospital and warn them I'll be taking at least a week off.' Her smile wavered and tears filled her eyes again. 'How *could* I have let this happen? I knew he was too young—too immature. I should have insisted he defer for a year.'

She was irresistible. With a muffled groan he swept her close to him again, wanting to stop her hurt and her fears as he had from that first time in the car park.

'Oh, my poor darling, don't blame yourself. You've done a magnificent job all these years. You can't be responsible for all the stupid mistakes your brother makes.'

For one delicious moment she flowed into him, yielding, accepting him. Her head found its rest where his head joined his shoulders. For one blissful moment he revelled in the feel of her in his arms, the familiar, delicate perfume that was Kaycee.

Her head willingly came up as he ran his hand over her head and tugged gently. He murmured incoherently as he stared into her soft brown eyes. But as he lowered his head to claim her lips, his whole body clamouring for all her sweetness, the softness vanished. The lithe body in his arms tensed. It seemed as though all the warmth fled from her and he knew that she had removed herself from him spiritually before she thrust him away physically.

'I won't stand for any more of your blow-hot, blow-cold treatment,' she said abruptly with scorn in her voice and her eyes.

Helplessly his arms fell away. She took a step back.

'Don't you ever dare touch me again. Even if Sonja Powers doesn't mind, I certainly do!'

CHAPTER ELEVEN

ROWAN stared at her consideringly. All expression had been wiped from his face at her angry words.

'Sonja, did you say?'

There was a mild tone to his voice but Kaycee blinked and nodded.

'I don't remember that I've ever mentioned her to you,' he mused even more gently. 'Been gossiping with Ken Rodgers, Nurse Wiseman?'

Fury flared through her. 'Oh, no, *Doctor* Scott, I haven't been listening to gossip. Not like you obviously have, seeing that Ken Rodgers is one of the best gossips in town. I've met the lady myself!' Then she added, without thinking, 'And I must say I'm not at all impressed with your choice of fiancée!'

There was dead silence. Rowan straightened suddenly. Kaycee saw his expression change and she took a step back.

'Fiancée, you say? Your opinion is very interesting. I'll make sure I tell my. . .er. . .fiancée that one day.'

Kaycee was reminded vividly of the first morning that she had met him. Then he had at first bellowed with pain, shouted at her and then lowered his voice. As now, there had been no mistaking the absolute fury in him despite his gentle tones.

'I take it Sonja's in town. Do you happen to know where she is now?'

His voice was still mild. As though he was asking nothing more interesting than what time it was. But a frigidity was there and icy fury flashed at her for one brief moment before he turned away.

'I suggested that if she required overnight accommodation she try the motel,' Kaycee was proud of her own indifferent tones. 'Of course, she may have gone back to the Rodgers place or even remained at the hospital.'

He was on his way to the door, his back squarely to her.

All Kaycee wanted to do was race after him. Beg him to love her. Only her. . .

Instead, she managed to say as casually as she could, 'Oh, by the way, the belongings of yours she brought from her flat are in my car.'

He paused for a brief moment and then swung around. She could read nothing from his expression.

'Oh, very good,' he said lightly. 'Especially since I didn't make it to Sydney myself, that'll save me a trip. I'll grab them on my way.'

Kaycee despised the solitary tear that trickled down her cheek. She knew that there were more where it had come from. Many more. She just wished that he would go and let her mourn her broken hopes and dreams in peace.

His face changed. The seething fury flared at her. 'Oh, Kaycee, you little idiot! Sonja Power is my ex-fiancée! Why on earth she told you anything else, I wouldn't have a clue.

'*And* your estimation of her character is way off beam. She's a very nice lady but we were never right for each other. Too different personalities; ideas about lifestyle, careers. . . We just never should have become engaged. It was all over between us a couple of years ago. But we still had to work together and have remained good friends.'

He took a step towards her but her eyes were blurred now with curtains of moisture. Through the drumming in her ears and heart another sound intruded. Only as Rowan swore shortly and sharply did she realise that it was the phone. He disappeared from her sight and she groped for a chair, collapsing onto it and burying her head in her hands.

She gave a dry, quivering sob. Could she dare believe him? If he had severed all romantic involvement with that confident woman she had met why did she still have so many of his things in her flat? But, then, wouldn't it be natural for a friend to store things. . .?

A few moments later Rowan reappeared. 'That was Ian Taylor.' His crisp, professional tones brought her head up sharply. 'He has a woman just going to Theatre for a Caesarean. Fortunately he has the anaesthetist from Taree there because a minibus has crashed in the mountains. The ambulance emergency centre has ordered the ambulance from Coolong to attend. It picked up John and is on its way but Ian thinks I should go, too.'

Only the many years of training came to Kaycee's rescue. She responded to him as one professional to another.

'Where is it?' When he told her, she said crisply, 'I'm coming, too.'

He started to protest but she strode forward. 'It's easy to take a wrong turn up there. I can show you the way as well as help when we get there. Do you have a warm jacket with you? It's always much colder that far up.'

She stopped and dismay filled her. 'Drew. Will he. . .?'

'Yes, he'll be all right,' Rowan said a trace

impatiently. 'He'll sleep for hours but leave a note in case. And if it's cold we'd better take extra blankets.'

Outside, her arms piled very high with woollen blankets, she started towards her car. A firm arm grabbed her and steered her away.

'We'll take mine,' Rowan said firmly as he relieved her of the blankets.

'But it's too low,' Kaycee protested. 'There are only gravel roads where. . .'

Then she remembered the four-wheel-drive wagon, just as they stopped beside it.

'I didn't think I'd be glad quite so quickly that I traded her in for this beauty,' Rowan said with satisfaction in his voice.

As they drove off Rowan filled her in quickly on all that Ian Taylor had been able to tell him. Apparently a twenty-seater minibus had rolled down a steep gully. A logging truck saw it happen and radioed on his two-way back to his base. They had rung the emergency 000 number. The ambulance centre for the region in Newcastle had gone into action but other vehicles from various centres would take much longer to reach the accident.

'Our church's seniors friendship group had an outing to the forest today,' Kaycee said steadily. 'They usually hire a minibus.'

Rowan glanced at her but didn't speak. Kaycee knew that it was useless speculating on what and who they would find.

The cleared farmland was behind them and the trees were getting taller and closer together before Kaycee said quietly, 'I thought you loved your sports car.'

Rowan shrugged carelessly. 'Sure did. It was a fun car to have and perhaps one day I'll be able to afford another one. But only as a second car. It wasn't practical for working in the country. And besides. . .' he paused and glanced at her '. . .It wasn't a family car. I've had this on order for a while. Picked it up this morning from the local dealer.'

Kaycee looked at him sadly and then away to stare blindly at the passing countryside. So this was confirmation of his intention to remain in Coolong.

But a family vehicle? Kaycee nervously chewed on her bottom lip. There was no reason to doubt what he had said about Sonja Powers. But why had the woman still called him her fiancée and why had Kaycee apparently been such a source of amusement to her?

She did not see him look across at her keenly but she heard him say, 'Kaycee, I meant what I said about Sonja Powers.'

Kaycee tensed defensively. 'She's really none of my business.'

She ventured a quick glance at him. His face looked very forbidding and his voice had sounded weary, even sad. There was silence for a moment and Kaycee felt the tension between them increase.

'You're right,' Rowan said crisply at last. 'She isn't any of your business. But she's none of mine, either. She hasn't been for a long time, except that we worked at the same hospital and she offered to store some of my things when I moved out of my flat. We won't talk about any of it now. I've been waiting until I moved out to talk to you. But we will talk.' His voice dropped. 'Oh, yes, we certainly will. And soon, very soon.'

Kaycee couldn't think of one thing to say. She wasn't sure if his last words had been a promise or a threat but they had sounded ominous, almost menacing.

There was a considerable pause before Rowan at

last asked abruptly, 'How much longer will it take to get there?'

Kaycee relaxed a little and was rather proud that her voice did not quiver as she replied, 'It depends whereabouts on that road they crashed. It goes for about forty kilometres and can take nearly an hour if the road's rough. Hopefully we're more than halfway.'

They continued in silence, with an occasional direction from Kaycee. Massive old gum-trees lined the narrow bitumen road winding its way higher and higher into the forests. At last the road petered out onto a dry, dusty gravel road.

'Why on earth would a minibus of senior citizens be travelling on this?' Rowan asked abruptly after several minutes of slowly negotiating a rough, winding road that badly needed grading.

'It's a popular area for short bush walks,' Kaycee said just as abruptly. 'The State Forest Commission maintains quite good picnic facilities further on.'

'Pity they don't maintain their roads better.'

'I'm sure they would if they were allowed to manage their forests properly without too much interference from radical greenies,' Kaycee snapped.

'You mean make a profit by chopping down all the old-growth trees for wood chipping?' Rowan said carelessly.

Kaycee flared. 'That's garbage promoted by ignorant—'

'Oh, dear,' Rowan interrupted mildly, 'the lady holds strong views on the issue.'

She subsided and, after a moment, said gruffly, 'Most people in Coolong do. I suggest you do some reading and studying to find out the real facts if you intend to live here.

'If some greenies have their way completely towns like Coolong that depend very heavily on the forest industry could become virtual ghost towns. And if the forests were being logged as irresponsibly as certain movements try to convince the rest of the country they are the industry would fold up.

'Anyway, what I've found after living here all my life is that, in most cases, the people working in the forests love them even more than the greenies. And that certainly goes for the foresters. I know a few of them in this area. They've got science degrees and their greatest desire is the long-term management and protection of the forests.

'I just wish they could be left to get on with the work they have spent years training to do. After all, what would we do without timber? I wish the powers that be would listen to them instead of to emotional. . .'

Kaycee broke off. They had slowly negotiated a sharp curve and an elderly woman was waving them down.

Rowan quickly explained to the grim-faced woman who they were and relief lit her anxious eyes. 'Just around the bend. They need all the help they can get.' She added rapidly, 'The local police arrived the same time as the ambulance did a few minutes ago. They've just radioed the State Emergency Services. A couple are trapped.'

She paused and her face crumpled. 'My husband and I arrived a little while after the accident. After radioing for help the driver of the jinker who found them had to get going so his load wouldn't block the rescue vehicles. There was only my husband and me until a few minutes ago. It's such a relief to see you all. It's a real mess down there.'

They couldn't see any of that yet as Rowan parked next behind the police and ambulance vehicles. He was waved over by a constable speaking into his radio mike.

When he had finished Rowan said briefly, 'Dr Scott and Nurse Wiseman, Coolong Hospital. What's the score?'

'I'm establishing a conversation and incident control communication link-up,' the grim-faced young officer said rapidly. 'The ambulance driver is just about finished assessing the injured. All are alive. . .' he swallowed '. . .so far. Two unconscious and trapped in the vehicle. Other injured are still in there. A few have been able to climb out.' His radio spluttered to life and he nodded briefly before turning away.

Rowan took a deep breath. 'Right, let's go.'

The lady was right. It was a mess. The minibus had rolled over before coming to rest against the huge trunk of a majestic old tree. A handful of people were lying or sitting on the sloping ground nearby. An elderly man was helping another over to the group.

'Just as well it left the road where it did and not over there.' Rowan muttered grimly.

Several metres further on a rocky cliff plunged away down a deep valley. The slope where they were was steep enough. Kaycee was glad of his firm hand as they picked their way carefully down and scrambled over to the battered vehicle. Fortunately, where it was lying the ground had levelled out a little.

John Swain backed out of the front section as they approached. Relief lightened his face a little as he saw Rowan. They peered into the vehicle at the elderly people strewn around in the mess of shattered glass and twisted metal. Some were lying quietly; others were groaning.

The ambulance officer was busy in the twisted body
of the vehicle. A policeman, leaning over a slumped
body at the front, looked up. He frowned but, before
he could speak, the ambulance man called, 'Good to
see you Doc, Kaycee.'

It was Bert, one of the senior officers who had run
the first-aid course Kaycee had attended. She gulped
as she saw several familiar faces, now pale and the
majority spattered with blood.

'Your church folk?' Rowan's compassionate voice
murmured in her ear.

She nodded, not trusting her voice. As soon as she
had seen the smashed vehicle she had known it was
the one from Coolong and that she would know many,
if not all, of the elderly people.

'Well, folks, not often we have two doctors and a
nurse come to help us,' Bert said loudly. 'And Nurse
Wiseman is a dab hand at applying splints and bandages. Taught her myself,' he added heartily, 'and she's
certainly the prettiest nurse at the hospital, so our
luck's in.'

He grinned around at the faces turned towards them
but when he turned back his eyes were anxious. He
lowered his voice and said rapidly, 'Fortunately the
vehicle's not on much of a slant so we've been able
to get to them and assess injuries. Several possible
fractures, a couple of minor head injuries, bad lacerations and a couple without evident external injuries
who appear badly shocked.'

He took a deep breath. 'The two up front are unconscious. Trapped. The driver's stuck between the
steering-wheel and the dashboard. The woman behind
him is in a pretty bad way, too. But we can't get to her
until some of these are moved. We'll just have to do

what we can until more help arrives. If you could brief your mate on those two up front, Dr Swain, I could use Kaycee here.'

The two men moved away. Kaycee heard John Swain quickly saying to Rowan, 'Crushed chest and possible other internals. We've started oxygen and. . .'

Rowan had started to crouch beside the blood-splattered figure when he stopped and looked back at Kaycee. Their eyes met in horrified communication.

'Think you can distribute those blankets around, Kaycee, and try to reassure them as much as you can?' Bert was murmuring.

She wrenched her attention away from the familiar body slumped between what had once been the wind-screen and the steering-wheel. It was Ken Rodgers.

'I know most of them, Bert,' Kaycee murmured back with an effort. 'That lady over there has been in hospital numerous times for stabilising her sugar levels.'

'Unstable diabetic. That's not what I wanted to hear,' he returned grimly. 'And there are no doubt a few more elderly with chronic health problems we'll have to watch out for. If you recognise anyone with a dicey heart condition you'd better let me know.'

The constable said something about securing the road for traffic and emergency vehicles and left them to it.

The time flew as Kaycee worked with Bert. She found herself helping to apply pressure bandages to severe cuts and splints to a couple of fractured arms and legs, constantly murmuring reassurances to the shocked and injured elderly people. Not one of the sixteen people had escaped some form of injury.

Rowan joined them after a little while. Kaycee looked across at him wordlessly.

He shook his head sadly. 'He's still alive, Kaycee.'
For one brief moment his hand touched her cheek and
his eyes caressed her lovingly. 'You're going great,
sweetheart,' he murmured encouragingly. Then he had
gone again, moving swiftly to the next person still
moaning with pain.

Her hand touched her face where his fingers had
scorched. Then, feeling immeasurably comforted and
fortified, she bent down to the frail old lady again.

It wasn't long before a couple of the more severely
injured people were manoeuvred onto stretchers and
placed side by side waiting to be lifted up to the
ambulance.

'Can't take them all the way up there away from
us until those other ambulances arrive from Stroud,
Dungog and Raymond Terrace,' Bert muttered out loud
before turning away and heading towards someone else
who had started to call out with pain.

One by one more ambulances arrived, as did the
SES. Kaycee silently admired the way the well-trained
personnel swung into action. Without fuss, the most
severely injured were whisked away to hospital first.

That did not include the two who had been trapped.
After being released by the SES team they had to wait
for the Hunter Westpac rescue helicopter from
Newcastle. Both doctors agreed that the woman with
spinal injuries should not risk the rough drive by road.

Rowan had come and updated Kaycee at the first
opportunity. 'Mr Rodgers is not to good, Kaycee,' he
said gently. 'Fortunately he's still unconscious or he'd
be in a lot of pain.'

Kaycee had fought back her horror as he went on to
say, 'I'm glad I had those chest X-rays done a few
weeks ago. He was fully recovered from his last bout

of infection but knowing he has emphysema only
means that we know he doesn't have a very good air
supply at the best of times. I'm pretty sure he has
a pneumothorax caused by at least one of his
fractured ribs.'

'But if one of his lungs have collapsed, what chance
has he?' Kaycee had whispered.

'He does have a chance,' Rowan had said emphatically, 'even if it's pretty slim. That old coot's a fighter
at the best of times. And, Kaycee, don't forget we've
been able to give him his chance.'

Before the helicopter arrived Ken Rodgers started to
regain consciousness. Kaycee had been sitting beside
him, monitoring his condition for Rowan, and called
to him softly.

'Right,' Rowan said grimly, 'I'll inject some pro-
caine local anaesthetic into the nerves above and below
the fractured ribs. It'll stop the worst of the pain so at
least he can breathe more deeply. Just try and stop him
moving about if he wakes up more.'

The old man stared up briefly at Kaycee. Recognition
flashed into his pain-filled eyes as she murmured to
him soothingly. But not long after he again became
unconscious, much to Kaycee's relief.

The sun had disappeared behind the mountains and
the light was fading rapidly before the distinctive sound
of the helicopter reached them. It was the new, large
helicopter and could hold four stretchers. Because the
road was too narrow and the trees too close to try and
land, the injured were winched up and delivered into
the care of the paramedic team on board.

'I wish you could have gone with Mr Rodgers,'
Kaycee said to Rowan as he joined her.

She felt his hand find and close gently around hers.

Her fingers curled and clung to him. His grip tightened.
He did not say a word as together they watched the big
bird-like machine lift up, swirl away over the treetops
and into the darkening sky to the helipad at the John
Hunter hospital in Newcastle.

'Too much to do back at Coolong with our share of
this lot,' Rowan said quietly at last as the noise faded
into the distance. 'John went with that first ambulance.
Come on, we'd better get back, too.'

Powerful lights had been erected and switched on as
dusk had descended. Still holding hands, they climbed
wearily back up to the road and out of their glare.
Kaycee began to realise how exhausted she was. Her
heart sank as the senior ambulance officer came over.

'Dr Scott, the last ambulance only has one man in
attendance. Would you mind travelling with him? He
can deliver to Coolong Hospital. Only a couple with
minor lacerations but one has a cardiac history and I
don't like the thought of only one officer with him.'

Rowan hesitated. 'But what about my vehicle and
Kaycee?'

'I can drive it,' Kaycee offered abruptly, hoping that
he could not see how disappointed she felt. She so
needed to spend time with him.

He stared at her doubtfully. 'It's almost dark. Ever
driven a four-wheel-drive wagon before?'

Kaycee shook her head.

Rowan looked anxious. 'Well, you won't need the
four-wheel drive on these roads but it's a long way and
you must be exhausted. Are you sure. . .?'

Kaycee knew that he was right. She was very tired
and his concern for her was all very nice but if he
didn't stop she would dissolve any moment into weak,

feminine tears and fling herself at him for comfort and strength.

She pulled away from him and deliberately put her hands on her hips. 'Of course I can drive your pride and treasure if I have to,' she said belligerently.

His eyes narrowed and then his exhausted, dirt-stained face lit up with a smile of sheer delight. 'I'm sure you can, sweetheart. I'm sure you can.'

Ignoring the waiting man, he leaned over and planted a smacking kiss straight on her lips.

'I love you, Kaycee Wiseman,' he said firmly, 'very, very much.'

For a moment he stared into her dazed eyes and then turned away, tossing over his shoulder, 'Come on, let's go home, sweetheart.'

The ambulance officer looked startled. Then he grinned and followed.

Kaycee didn't move.

Had he really said he loved her?

'Kaycee!'

At the exasperated bellow she jumped and started forward.

Rowan's eyes twinkled at her as he tossed her a key. 'Call me at the hospital when you get home.'

Then he was gone.

The lights started flashing on top of the ambulance as it pulled slowly away. For a moment she watched it and then headed for the wagon.

He had said that he loved her.

He had called her 'sweetheart'. And more than once during the last few hours, she suddenly recalled. And he had called her 'love'. He was saying the right words. Words that tingled through her. Words that she longed to be free to say back to him.

Perhaps she could.

She automatically familiarised herself with the dashboard and inserted the key in the ignition. Hope
continued to grow and a smile tilted her lips. Then
it faded.

Suddenly she rested her head on her hands on the
steering-wheel. But did she love him enough to live
where he wanted to live? Did he love her enough to be
able to accept what she felt about the country—about
Coolong?

Several times during the last few torrid hours she
had been conscious of him watching over her. Nothing
had been said. There had been a quick smile of encour-
agement across the space separating them as they both
attended an accident victim.

Once, after she had held the arm of a confused,
pain-racked old lady while he slipped in the injection
of morphia, she had felt his brief, tender touch on her
own hand. Another time she had raced to tell him that
someone was feeling very nauseous and needed max-
alon. His quiet smile and 'Good girl' had caused a rush
of pleasure to sweep through her.

Despite the horror all around there had been an inti-
macy between them—that silent communication that
she suddenly knew had dispensed strength and comfort
to them both.

They could work things out.

The sudden conviction swept through her like wild-
fire. She raised her head and smiled again.

It was a lonely trip home but she was buoyed up with
excitement, with anticipation. She was only a couple of
kilometres from Coolong outskirts when a dark shape
moved in the glare of her headlights. Fortunately she
was not travelling very fast. As the cow lumbered onto

the road Kaycee hit the brakes. There was a screech of
tyres. The vehicle went into a skid and then jolted
sideways into the deep ditch at the side of the road.

Rowan glanced up at the clock on the wall for the
hundredth time. His lips tightened. Kaycee should have
been safely home an hour ago. Why hadn't she phoned?

Fear gripped him as it never had before. Had he been
mistaken after all? Was her anger and hurt about Sonja
not because she loved him, too, as he had decided some
time during the nightmare in the forest? Or had she not
called because something had happened? Could she
have lost control on those tortuous bends? Gone to
sleep at the wheel?

Anguish twisted a knot deep inside him so that he
winced.

'Are you all right, Rowan?'

Sonja Power's soft voice reached him through his
haze of worry and exhaustion. She had just completed
cleaning and suturing a cut on the leg of the same
patient whose fractured arm he had reduced and was
now plastering.

He looked up at her. 'I'm tired,' he said flatly.

'And worried, I think, my friend?' She watched him
for a moment and then added compassionately, 'I'm
really sorry your friend Ken Rodgers didn't make it.'

'Kaycee's going to be very upset,' he muttered after
controlling the lump in his throat at the thought of the
old man.

Word had come through not so very long ago that
he had died shortly after admission to hospital. He
glanced up again at the clock. Had Kaycee heard
already? But why hadn't she phoned him? Surely she
knew he would be worried.

Rowan mechanically finished smoothing his wet hands over the white, slippery surface. He forced a smile at the old, snowy-haired man who stared up at them from drugged eyes.

'There you are, Mr Linton. You'd better spend the night in hospital for the nurses to keep an eye on you while that dries.'

The man closed his eyes again as Rowan moved away. 'Well, that's the last one for me. It was good of you to stay and help out, Sonja,' he said formally, 'otherwise it would have taken us much longer.'

She shrugged. 'Glad I was here. It was really hectic there for a while before you arrived back. Certainly hasn't been my idea of what quiet life in a small country hospital is like.'

The surprise in her voice made him smile slightly. Then he remembered what Kaycee had said about the similarities of working in any size hospital. Once again his eyes flew to the clock.

'For goodness' sake, Rowan,' Sonja exclaimed impatiently, 'if you feel like this about the girl I, for the life of me, don't know why you think she doesn't feel the same about you.' She actually snorted and added peevishly, 'One look at the girl when I told her I was your fiancée and I knew you were mad not to see it.'

He stopped clearing away and suddenly swung around and glared at her. 'What on earth got into you that made you tell Kaycee and that receptionist you were my fiancée? It wasn't very pleasant having Sister Allen inform me that my fiancée was here in the way she did.'

'That receptionist was so darned wary about giving out your private address.' Sonja suddenly grinned at him. 'It really upset the apple-cart, didn't it? Especially that old girl! Your Kaycee must be very popular. Is she really your fiancée, like everybody thinks?'

He scowled at her. 'It's not a bit funny. Sister Joan Allen has become a good friend. And Kaycee's not my fiancée.' He took a deep breath and began meaningfully, 'Not yet but I hope——'

The sound of a heavy vehicle pulling up quickly outside made him break off and listen intently. There was the slam of a door and then a voice calling his name.

Like a rocket he was racing towards the entrance, slamming to a halt as the sliding doors opened and a bedraggled, filthy figure hove into sight.

Relief and fury in equal measure overwhelmed him. 'Why didn't you ring me? Where the hell have you been?' he yelled furiously and started forward again. Then he took a second look at her and his breath left him. 'Kaycee. . . You. . . What. . .?'

She had paused momentarily at the sight of him. Then she kept coming and he noticed that she limped slightly. To his added horror a tiny dribble of blood trickled from her cheek to disappear down the neck of her indescribable dress that had once been a nurse's uniform.

'I've been trying not to hit a cow, that's what I've been doing,' she yelled right back at him. A finger poked into his chest as the words kept roaring out. 'I love you, too, Rowan Scott. And don't you dare shout at me! I've smashed your new car!'

Then she spotted Sonja as she appeared beside him. Redress swept into her white, exhausted face. 'And just what are you still doing here? He's not your fiancée; he's mine,' she said furiously.

There was dead silence.

And then several things happened at once.

Kaycee's legs gave out. She wilted against him and Rowan swept her into his arms.

The voice of Sister Allen said sternly, 'I'm very glad to hear it, Nurse Wiseman.'

There was a peal of laughter from Sonja. 'And you told me you wanted a change of pace to the slower, quieter countryside, Rowan!'

But Rowan was oblivious to all but the precious bundle in his arms. He lifted her up and made for one of the recently vacated cubicles.

'Kaycee, are you hurt, my darling?'

'Oh, Rowan,' she wailed as she clutched him, 'I put your new car in the ditch and all the nice new paint's all dented and scratched and I didn't know how to engage the four-wheel drive and I was stuck there until that nice policeman from the accident came along and then a truck pulled me out and I knew you'd be worried and. . .'

'Hush, now, sweetheart,' he rocked her tenderly. 'Nothing matters except that you're here now and you aren't too badly hurt.'

She sniffled and buried her face deeper in his shoulder. Her voice was muffled. 'I'm not hurt. I scratched my face and leg on a shrub when I climbed out of the ditch.'

Relief swamped him and he closed his eyes on a deep sigh. He hugged her even more tightly and then lifted up her face. He searched the tear-drenched, exhausted eyes anxiously and then relaxed even more. Reaching over, he grabbed a handful of tissues and very, very gently wiped her face.

'Are you really my fiancée, Kaycee?'

He felt her tense and added very carefully, 'You see, I really meant to ask you to marry me this evening after I knew for certain I had a job as superintendent at a hospital.'

Her eyes widened and her mouth dropped. Colour flooded her face.

'You see,' he continued swiftly, 'the job's not in the huge city of Sydney and it's not in as small a town as Coolong. Newcastle's not a bad size for a big city. This hospital's close enough to Newcastle so you can enjoy a city and all your art courses or whatever your heart desires. You can keep a closer eye on Drew. He could even stay with us.'

He paused for breath and then rushed on as she went to speak. 'But the hospital's still in a nearby country town—nowhere near as big as even Newcastle but bigger than Coolong. After a couple of years I could go into private practice there if that's what we decide. We can buy an acreage not too far away so I can enjoy the atmosphere of the bush.

'But I also want to buy your old house here so that we can come back to Coolong some time if we don't like it there after all. Your mother and I have already talked about the possibility. I've fallen in love with this area and, after all, it's only a couple of hours away.'

He stared at her anxiously as the spate of words dried up. Kaycee opened and shut her mouth a couple of times.

'You. . .you never mentioned marriage, did you?' she said at last in a small voice.

'Well, no. As a matter of fact I haven't dared trust myself too much. . .' He paused and suddenly glanced over his shoulder.

He glared and then raised his voice quite loudly. 'I

loved you so much it was torture living in the same house like we were, trying *not* to have that affair everyone was so sure we were already enjoying. Then the gossips would have been proved right,' he added even more loudly and scowled at the circle of fascinated faces watching avidly.

Kaycee followed his glance. Suddenly she pushed herself upright. 'It's quite all right, Rowan. I don't mind in the least what anyone says any more.'

She didn't see the proud, tender look that filled his face as she surveyed the whole evening staff of Accident and Emergency. Her eyes lingered on the wide-eyed, gaping Sonja Power.

'You see,' she announced coolly, 'it doesn't really matter much where we live as long as we do it together.'

She paused as a muffled sound came from Rowan. She frowned at him and then turned back to their audience. 'Dr Scott and I love each other and are going to be married. Not that it's anybody else's business but his and mine but it looks as though we won't be living in Coolong for a while, if ever.'

'Er, sweetheart,' Rowan murmured gently, his eyes dancing, 'they already know.'

She looked at him, and then surveyed them all again. Crossly this time. 'Then why are you all gaping at us like that?'

Sister Allen folded her arms on her ample bosom. 'Really Nurse Wiseman,' she snapped, 'because we're all hoping you'll kiss each other and get it over with.'

Rowan stood up with his arms still tightly wrapped around Kaycee. They started towards the exit. Love had transformed each exhausted face as they marched past them all.

Near the outside door Rowan paused. 'Our car is drivable, isn't it?'

Speechless, Kaycee nodded, her eyes adoring him for his tenderness and the love in his face.

He turned and faced the bemused, grinning staff. Sonja was actually giggling.

'We're going to kiss each other when and where and how we want to,' he stated calmly. 'But, I can tell you now, it's going to happen very, very frequently, very privately and for the rest of our lives.'

He gave a mock bow and then the entwined couple disappeared slowly from sight, totally absorbed in each other.

Neither heard Sister Allen have the last word.

'Well, that's that I suppose,' she said with an air of some disappointment. Then she straightened and even Sonja Power clicked to attention. 'Thank goodness that's settled and over at last. Now, hop to it! Let's get this place cleaned up and ready for the next patient!'

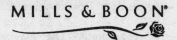

MILLS & BOON®

Medical Romance™

Books for enjoyment this month...

CRISIS FOR CASSANDRA	Abigail Gordon
PRESCRIPTION—ONE HUSBAND	Marion Lennox
WORTH WAITING FOR	Josie Metcalfe
DR RYDER AND SON	Gill Sanderson

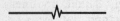 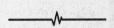

Treats in store!

Watch next month for these absorbing stories...

TRUSTING DR SCOTT	Mary Hawkins
PRESCRIPTION—ONE BRIDE	Marion Lennox
TAKING RISKS	Sharon Kendrick
PERFECT PRESCRIPTION	Carol Wood

GET 4 BOOKS
AND A SILVER PLATED
PHOTO FRAME

Return this coupon and we'll send you 4 Mills & Boon Medical Romance™ novels and a silver plated photo frame absolutely FREE! We'll even pay the postage and packing for you.

We're making you this offer to introduce you to the benefits of Reader Service: FREE home delivery of brand-new Mills & Boon Medical Romance novels, at least a month before they are available in the shops, FREE gifts and a monthly Newsletter packed with information.

Accepting these FREE books and gift places you under no obligation to buy, you may cancel at any time, even after receiving just your free shipment. Simply complete the coupon below and send it to:

MILLS & BOON® READER SERVICE, FREEPOST, CROYDON, SURREY, CR9 3WZ.

No stamp needed

Yes, please send me 4 free Mills & Boon Medical Romance novels and a silver plated photo frame. I understand that unless you hear from me, I will receive 4 superb new titles every month for just £2.10* each postage and packing free. I am under no obligation to purchase any books and I may cancel or suspend my subscription at any time, but the free books and gifts will be mine to keep in any case. (I am over 18 years of age)

M6IE

Ms/Mrs/Miss/Mr _____

Address _____

_____

_____ Postcode _____